Finding Christmas
by

Kathi Daley

This book is a work of fiction. Names, characters, places, and incidents either are products of the author's imagination or are used fictitiously. Any resemblance to actual events or locales or persons, living or dead, is entirely coincidental.

Copyright © 2018 by Katherine Daley

Version 1.0

All rights reserved, including the right of reproduction in whole or in part in any form.

Chapter 1

Saturday, December 15

The short days of winter had set in, creating a state of almost perpetual darkness. When combined with the heavy clouds that had blanketed the area for the past week, I was beginning to think the sun had disappeared completely. Having lived in Rescue, Alaska, my entire life, I'd learned to roll with the changing weather, but for some reason, this year the endless snow and dark skies were beginning to get on my nerves. Not that there was a thing I could do about the weather, I reminded myself as I handed out event tickets to the sugared-up children at the annual Winter Wonderland Christmas Celebration.

"You do realize that since we've been here, Grandma has been run over by a reindeer at least three times, Frosty has stolen some poor guy's hat at least twice, Rudolph has been bullied by his nasally unimpaired classmates a whopping six times, and the

Grinch has stolen Christmas despite the fact that my own powers of observation tell me Christmas is alive and well."

I glanced at my ticket booth partner, Officer Hank Houston. He hadn't wanted to participate in this annual event when I'd first approached him about it, but over time, my tenacious nagging had worn him down and he'd agreed to help me with the shift my best friend, Chloe Rivers, had badgered me into signing up for. "I take it you aren't a fan of the kiddie carols Chloe put on an endless loop from hell."

Houston ran his hands through his thick brown hair. "It's not that I have anything against the carols per se, it's just that Christmas isn't really my thing. I guess all the ho-ho-hos and one-horse open sleighs are getting to me. How long is this shift?"

"Four hours."

"And how long have we been here?"

"One hour."

I tried unsuccessfully to suppress a smile as Houston let out a very unmanly groan.

"You sound like you're dying." I chuckled. "It really isn't that bad."

"Isn't it?"

I raised a brow. "Okay, this is a bit much, but I'm going to go out on a limb and assume it isn't just the noise and the chaos. If I had to guess I'd say there is a deep psychological reason you aren't a fan of the jolly old man in red."

Houston shrugged. "It's not that I am some sort of a Grinch but I will admit the big guy and I have had a few problems over the years."

"I see. Do you want to talk about it?"

"Not really. Are you sure you need me to help you? It's my day off, barring any emergencies, and it seems like you have this under control."

I was debating whether to let Houston off the hook when I noticed the very real pain in his eyes. Maybe he really wasn't being a Grinch. I knew he'd moved to Rescue the previous spring after having suffered a personal tragedy he was unwilling to talk about. Now, if I had to guess, that tragedy was Christmas involved, given his lack of enthusiasm for the holiday. "I get the aversion to the hoopla," I said with compassion. "I haven't always been the biggest lover of the season myself."

Houston frowned. "I'm sorry. I remember you mentioning your parents died in a car accident at Christmas."

I shrugged. "I'm fine. I've mostly been able to move past it." That wasn't totally true, but I liked to tell myself it was.

Houston opened his mouth as if to reply when a woman dressed as an elf came over to us. "Are you Harmony Carson?"

"I am," I answered.

"I have a message for you from a man named Jake Cartwright."

Jake was my boss and brother-in-law. "I wonder why he didn't just call my cell." I pulled it out of my pocket and looked at it. No bars.

The elf replied, "The man I spoke to called the landline we set up for this event when he couldn't get hold of your cell. He said the team has been called out on a rescue. He needs you to meet him at the Rescue Inn as soon as you can get there. And he said to bring Yukon." The elf, who must be new in town because

I'd never met her and she didn't seem to know who either Jake or I were, glanced at Houston with an appreciative gleam in her eye. "I don't suppose you're Yukon?"

Houston laughed. "Hardly. I'm Hank Houston. Yukon is a dog," He looked at me with what could only be an expression of relief on his face. "It sounds like duty calls. Carl is on shift today, but a search-and-rescue call sounds like something I should handle personally."

I found I had to agree. Carl Flanders and Donny Quinlan, the deputies Houston had inherited when he'd taken on the job as police chief, weren't exactly the most motivated men in the world. They provided somewhat adequate support when it came to day-to-day tasks, but they certainly weren't the men you'd want in charge during an emergency, which, if you thought about it, was pretty ironic given that responding to emergencies was pretty much their entire job description.

I picked up the backpack I used as a purse and nodded at Houston. "If you're coming, grab your stuff. I'm already out of here."

"But you can't both leave," the elf complained as Houston began gathering his own hat, coat, and gloves. "Who'll man the ticket booth?"

I handed the cashbox to the woman who wore little more than green tights and some sort of short red dress that barely covered the tops of her thighs. "I'm sure you can handle things until the next shift gets here in three hours." With that, I grabbed Houston's hand and headed toward the exit before anyone came up with a reason to cause us to stay.

******

The search-and-rescue team had been called out to find an elderly man who'd been staying with his daughter and son-in-law at the Rescue Inn. He hadn't been seen since he went up to bed at nine thirty the previous evening, so we weren't sure how long he'd been out in the snow dressed in nothing but his furry red Santa suit. It was almost eleven a.m. now, and the temperature was hovering around zero. If he'd been out in the cold for more than a couple of hours, I was afraid this was going to be a retrieval operation rather than a rescue.

According to Jake, our victim was a seventy-six-year-old named Nick Clauston. Nick's daughter, Noel Snow, had reported her father missing at around ten fifteen that morning. He hadn't come down to breakfast, but initially, she hadn't worried because he slept late and it wasn't unusual for him to skip breakfast altogether. When he hadn't come downstairs by ten o'clock, she went up to his room to check on him. She found he was gone from his room, as was his red Santa suit. She looked around the inn and its immediate area and when he wasn't found, Mrs. Snow called Carl at the police station, who referred her to Jake. Noel told him she had no idea whether her father had wandered off that morning or during the night, although she suspected it might have been this morning because she didn't think it likely he would leave the inn when it was pitch black outside. I certainly hoped that was the case.

"Jake to Harmony," I heard through the two-way radio I carried as I trudged on snowshoes through drifts of deep snow. My search-and-rescue dog

Yukon and I had been paired with fellow S&R team member Wyatt Forrester.

I paused, wiping a huge snowflake from my cheek before I answered. "Go for Harmony."

"Sitka seems to have lost the scent." Jake, who served as the leader of the search-and-rescue team, referred to our lead search and rescue dog. "Initially it seemed like he had something, but at this point he just looks confused. Do you and Yukon have anything?"

"It seemed Yukon had a scent when we first started out, but he seems to have lost it as well," I answered. I looked around at the dense forest. "It's snowed quite a bit in the past few hours. If the man came this way, it's likely his tracks will be covered."

"Any luck making a connection?"

"No." I looked around at the blanket of white. "I'll try again." The team depended on my ability to psychically connect to victims I was meant to help rescue. My ability, which I oftentimes considered a curse, had come to me during the lowest point in my life. My sister Val, who had become my guardian after our parents died, had gone out on a rescue. She'd become lost in a storm, and although the team tried to find her, they came up with nothing but dead ends. She was the first person I connected to, and the one I most wanted to save. I couldn't save Val, but since then, I'd used my gift to locate and rescue dozens of people.

I found a large rock, brushed off the snow, and sat down. I focused in on the photo of the white-haired man with rosy red cheeks dressed in a very authentic-looking Santa costume. His daughter had told us they'd come to Rescue so her husband could ski, but ultimately, they'd chosen Alaska as their vacation destination so her father could participate in the Santa Festival being held in Tinseltown, only a short drive from Rescue. Well, it was a short drive by Alaska standards. It was a little more than an hour away.

Mrs. Snow had explained that Mr. Clauston suffered from the early stages of dementia, although he seemed to be having a lot of good days lately, and she felt he was doing much better than he was when he was first diagnosed. She had real hope the progression of his disease had been stalled, at least until she'd discovered he'd wandered away without his snow boots or heavy jacket.

I closed my eyes and focused on the man's jolly face. I tried to think as he would, which I hoped would increase my odds of making a connection. Mrs. Snow had told us that at times, her father actually believed he was Santa Claus and behaved accordingly. He'd do things that in his mind Santa would do. For example, not long ago, her father had collected a bunch of stuff he had around his house, wrapped it, and broke into houses up and down the block where he lived, delivering gifts.

Making a connection to a person in need of rescue is far from an exact science. Sometimes their image comes through clearly, while at others, it doesn't come through at all. I knew not to force it. I simply let the images that presented themselves caress my mind. I could hear Yukon panting next to me and Wyatt moving around, but I forced my mind to be still and settle down. I pulled up an image of rosy cheeks, faded blue eyes, white hair, a lopsided smile, and a mind filled with the possibility of magic.

"I might have something," I said after a minute of intense concentration. "Although to be honest, the vision is vague. I can't make out any details."

"What are you picking up?" Jake asked through the radio.

"I sense hay. Maybe a barn?"

"I suppose Mr. Clauston might have sought out shelter in a barn," Jake said. "With all the fresh snow, he couldn't have gotten too far from the inn, though, and I can't think of any barns in the immediate area."

"Yeah." I frowned. "The image of the barn doesn't really fit." I took a deep breath and tried to focus deeper. I could sense Yukon was becoming restless at the delay. I was sure Jake, Sitka, and Landon were restless waiting for me to do my thing as well, and that just made me tense and less able to focus.

I thought back to the interview we'd had with Noel Snow when we'd responded to the call. Houston had taken over from Jake, asking the questions one would ask with any missing persons case. Why had the family been visiting Rescue? How long had the man been missing? What might he have been wearing or taken with him? And how might he have left the area? Houston wondered whether Nick Clauston had access to a vehicle or if it was more likely he had set off on foot. When his daughter said he hadn't had access to a vehicle, Houston asked if he might have hitchhiked. She didn't think he would have, and there was very little traffic on the road where the inn was located, so it was most likely he'd remained within walking distance of the inn. The poor woman had been so upset. I wanted to find her father, but other than the faint sense of him being associated with hay, I had nothing.

I was about to give up when a flash of an elderly man with a white beard that reached the middle of his chest brushed across my mind. "I think I have him," I whispered. "I'm still picking up on the hay, but the image is stronger now. There's something else." I focused in. "A sleigh."

"Where?" Jake asked.

I bit my lip. "I'm not sure."

I released the button on the radio and let my hand and body relax. The image I'd captured felt just out of my reach. The vision was more of a flash of insight. I didn't sense the man was frightened or in any immediate danger. In fact, I was pretty sure he was having a jolly good time.

"We did see those sleigh tracks a ways back," Wyatt reminded me after a few minutes.

I opened my eyes. "You're right." I pressed the button on the radio again. "Harmony to Jake."

"Go for Jake."

"Wyatt and I are going to backtrack. We saw sleigh tracks a ways back. We didn't think much about them because Mr. Clauston's daughter didn't mention a sleigh, but I think we should follow them to see where they lead."

"Send me your coordinates and we'll join you."

Wyatt sent Jake the coordinates and we headed back the way we'd come. Once we arrived at the place where we remembered seeing the tracks, I paused to give Yukon the old man's scent. I took the shirt his daughter had provided from the plastic bag I carried it in and prayed he would pick up the trail again. "This is Nick Clauston," I said to Yukon. "Find Nick."

Yukon sniffed the shirt, then began to sniff the air. At first, he didn't seem to have found the scent, but after a few minutes, he headed out.

"How do you think sleigh tracks might fit into his disappearance?" Wyatt asked as we trudged through the deep snow, following Yukon.

"I don't know. Maybe someone found him. Someone in a sleigh. Maybe he couldn't remember where he was supposed to be, so the person in the sleigh took him back to their barn."

Wyatt looked doubtful. "If you found a man wandering around in the snow dressed in a Santa suit who couldn't remember where he was supposed to be, wouldn't you call the police?"

I let out a breath. "Yeah, I guess I would. To be honest I have no idea how the sleigh or the barn fits into this whole thing. All I do know is that when I focused on Mr. Clauston, that is the image that came to me."

Wyatt and I continued to trudge along. It was difficult to walk with so many drifts, so we leaned forward and looked at the ground directly in front of us as we made our way. Eventually I heard Wyatt say, "Yukon is alerting." He walked forward a bit more. "It looks like he found the tracks we saw earlier."

I radioed Jake that we were back to the point we were looking for, and he radioed for us to wait. He and Landon were only a minute or two away from us. I used the wait time to catch my breath. Walking the rough terrain in snowshoes large enough to provide traction in deep snow wasn't an easy task.

Once Jake and Landon caught up with us, we slowly made our way forward, trying our best to follow tracks that disappeared into drifts only to reappear again on the other side.

At one point, Wyatt stopped and knelt down for a closer look. We were somewhat protected from the wind here, so the drifts weren't as deep. "There are hoofprints in the snow as well as sleigh tracks, but there aren't any horse prints."

I walked over to where he was standing. It did look like a sleigh pulled by an animal had been through here. "Caribou," I said after studying the two distinct toes.

Wyatt chuckled. "So, you're saying a man dressed in a Santa suit was picked up in a sleigh pulled by reindeer."

I smiled in return. "That's what the evidence suggests." The dogs seemed to have picked up a scent and gone on ahead. Eventually, they stopped walking and looked around. I paused to study the tracks left in the snow. "A sleigh pulled by caribou definitely traveled through here. It seems the sleigh tracks end at the edge of the forest."

"Maybe Santa's magic reindeer took flight once they came to the edge of the meadow," Wyatt teased.

My lips curled into a half smile. "Again, that would seem to be what the evidence suggests."

"I'm sure if we try hard enough, we can come up with an explanation based in reality," Landon countered.

"Perhaps." I took several steps into the woods at the edge of the clearing. I paused, listened, and looked around. I had the distinct feeling we were being watched, but I didn't see or hear anything.

"Do you sense something?" Jake asked.

I shook my head. "I don't know. I feel something, but I'm not sure it's him. I think maybe..." I was cut off by the sound of Jake's phone.

Jake lifted a finger to quiet me so he could answer. "Jake here." Jake raised a brow. "Really? Well, thanks for letting us know." Jake hung up and turned toward us. "It seems Nick is back at the inn."

I narrowed my gaze. "How did he get there?"

"No one's sure. Houston went outside to get something from his squad car and found Nick sitting on the porch swing near the front door. When he asked him where he'd been and how he'd gotten back to the inn, Mr. Clauston told Houston he woke up during the night and saw lights in the sky. He went outside to take a look and got lost. He was just starting to get worried when Santa appeared in a sleigh pulled by two reindeer. He offered to give him a ride home, but when he couldn't remember where home was, Santa took him to his reindeer barn. He gave him a cup of cocoa and a warm blanket and talked to him a bit. Eventually, Mr. Clauston remembered the inn, and Santa brought him back and dropped him off."

"Hot damn," Wyatt said. "I knew Santa was involved in this."

"There's no such thing as Santa," Landon argued.

"I think it's likely the man was hallucinating," Jake said.

"I might agree if not for the sleigh tracks and the reindeer hooves," I countered. "Maybe Wyatt's right. Maybe Mr. Clauston really *was* rescued by Santa."

Jake rolled his eyes. "This is northern Alaska. A lot of people have sleighs, and a fair number have domesticated caribou. I'm sure what he saw were the northern lights and the Santa who picked him up was a Good Samaritan out for a sleigh ride."

"Who, other than Santa of course, goes for a sleigh ride in the middle of the night?" I queried.

"Yeah, who?" Wyatt laughed.

Jake started walking back the way we'd come. I didn't actually believe Mr. Clauston had been saved by Santa, but it was fun messing with Jake and Landon, who were so steadfast in their disbelief. I didn't know who had saved him; I was just glad he was okay.

Chapter 2

After we returned to the inn, Jake spoke to Nick Clauston's daughter, while Wyatt, Landon, and I gathered our stuff and began loading the trucks. Marty and Mary Miller, the owners of the inn, had done a wonderful job decorating. Not only was the outside of the building decked out in lights, but the interior of the cozy lodging had been strung with lights and garlands as well. I could see why the place was so popular with the holiday crowd. Staying at the inn must be a bit like spending the holiday at Santa's magical workshop.

"The place looks nice," Landon said as he passed the spot where I'd paused to admire the fifteen-foot tree.

"It's really beautiful," I answered and stuffed down a longing in my heart. "Before she died, my mom used to decorate a tree much like this one. I can still remember the colorful lights and the whisper of

Christmas as I curled up on the floor, looking up through the branches."

"It sounds nice," Landon replied as I continued to gaze at the tree.

I sighed as the memories came flooding forth. "It was magical. My mom really understood the importance of the season and worked hard to make everything perfect. When I allow my mind to drift into the past, I can almost hear the carols on the stereo, smell the pinesap from the tree, and see the shiny red bulbs reflecting my image as I waited for Santa."

Landon took a step closer and put his arm around my shoulder. He gave my arm a squeeze as we stood in silence and continued to look at the tree. White lights twinkled and danced like stars on a clear winter night. I let out a soft breath as I rested my head on his shoulder. "I love the pine cones that have been placed around the bright red bulbs and white lights to give the tree an outdoorsy feel."

"Have you put up a tree yet this year?" Landon asked.

I took a slight step away and shook my head. It wasn't like me to be quite so sappy. Practical, I reminded myself, was more my style. "I thought about it, but I don't have extra cash to buy decorations, and a tree without decorations would be nothing more than an invitation for the dogs to pee on it and the cats to climb it."

Landon's eyes grew large, as if a light bulb suddenly went on. "Your decorations were stored in the barn."

I nodded. "I didn't have many to begin with, but the ones I did have were in the barn when it burned.

It's fine, though. Jake went crazy decorating the bar this year, so I can get my Christmas jollies while I'm at work."

I turned back toward the front door. "I'll grab Yukon. Jake looks like he's almost done talking to Marty and Mary, and I'm sure he'll want to get on with our own debriefing."

Landon nodded and, picking up the backpack with the supplies we'd brought with us, he headed out to Jake's truck. I'd picked up my own Jeep when I'd gone home to get Yukon, so I decided to drop him back at home before meeting Jake and the others at Neverland.

"Other than the Santa factor, does anyone have anything to add that may prove to be unique to this case? Anything we might want to keep in mind for future rescues?" Jake asked the standard questions that followed during every debriefing, even though this rescue had turned out to be pretty tame.

We agreed that nothing out of the ordinary had occurred and were just happy that Mr. Clauston had been returned to the inn in one piece, however it happened.

When Jake had asked all the questions he needed for the report, I went over to the Rescue Animal Shelter. We planned to decorate that day and I didn't want to miss the party. By the time I arrived, Harley Medford, our benefactor, had already hung the lights along the roofline. The red and white lights against the white snow and dark gray sky gave the place a festive feel that did a lot to chase away the ho-hums I'd been experiencing lately.

"It looks great." I walked over and stood next to Serena Walters, one of the shelter volunteers, who was holding the ladder and handing Harley, who was wearing a fuzzy Santa hat, C9 replacement bulbs.

"When Harley Medford does Christmas, Christmas knows it's been done." Harley chuckled.

I rolled my eyes. "For someone who makes a living delivering the perfect line at the perfect time, that was really corny."

He laughed as he screwed a white light into the empty socket next to a red one. "Maybe, but you have to admit the place is looking pretty festive." Harley climbed down the ladder, then stood back to admire his work.

"It really does," I said as we admired the lights. "And the Santa on the roof with the eight dogs pulling the sleigh is adorable. Where did you get them anyway?"

"Special order. I wanted the shelter to really stand out. The lights are great, but the sleigh with the dogs gives the place character as well as identity."

"I'd say we have a very good chance at winning the competition the chamber is hosting."

"That's the plan." Harley crossed his arms and gazed at the building. "I still need to put lights around the windows, and I don't want to forget the wreaths I picked up in town." He turned and headed to his truck, with Serena and me tagging along behind. It was less than two weeks until Christmas and the whole town of Rescue had gone just a bit Christmas crazy. It had started when Jake went all-out decorating Neverland. Other businesses around town decided to try to outdo his efforts, and the first-ever Rescue, Alaska decorating war was born. When the gang at the animal shelter decided we needed to take part, we were fortunate to have Harley announce he was all-in and not only provided the funds to buy the decorations but the labor to put them up too.

"How did the rescue go?" Harley asked.

"Well. It turned out the man who thought he was Santa was rescued by the man himself."

"Huh?" Serena said as Harley began handing her wreathes to carry.

I took a minute to fill them in.

"That's kind of fun in a ten-days-before-Christmas way." Serena's eyes danced with merriment as she spoke.

"That's what Wyatt and I thought. Of course, Landon and Jake were all practical, with their there's-no-such-thing-as-Santa response."

"That isn't surprising. Landon especially is Mr. Logic," Serena said.

"As fun as the thought of the real Santa rescuing a lost man dressed as Santa is, I wonder who actually rescued him," Harley said. "Isn't it a little odd that this Good Samaritan dropped him off outside rather than bringing him in?"

I frowned as Harley loaded me up with wreaths too. "I guess it is. Mr. Clauston was obviously confused. It does seem whoever brought him back to the inn would want to make sure he was safe, with people who would look out for him."

"Unless it really *was* Santa and he didn't want to blow his cover." Serena giggled. "Speaking of Santa, did you volunteer at the Christmas Festival as you planned?"

"For a while," I answered. "I signed up for a four-hour shift but was called in on the rescue after the first hour."

"How was the festival?" Serena asked.

"Fun, in an overdone way."

Serena raised a brow. "Overdone?"

"It was just a lot. A lot of people, a lot of decorations, a lot of music, and a lot of food. Everyone looked as if they were having fun, though. Are you still volunteering tomorrow?"

Serena smiled. "Yes. And I'm really looking forward to it."

"I never did get around to signing up for a shift," Harley said. "But I'd like to go. Is it going on all weekend?"

"Until five o'clock tomorrow," I confirmed.

"I don't suppose you want to come along and show me around?" Harley asked.

I shrugged. "Sure. I can do that. Just let me know what time you want to go."

"I'll text you."

I set the last load of wreaths on the reception desk and stood back to take it all in. The shelter was going to be more festively decorated than the North Pole if Harley had his way.

"It looks like the couple who are adopting the malamute we took in last week are here," Serena said after she set the wreaths in her arms on the counter next to mine. "I'll go talk to them. Be sure to save a few wreaths for the reception area."

"We should string lights inside as well," I added as Serena began to walk away.

"There are boxes of lights in the office," she said over her shoulder.

I picked up one of the wreaths and began tying on a bow from the spool of thick red ribbon Harley had bought. "Maybe we should wrap the front door like a present. It's protected from all but a direct northerly, so it probably won't get ruined in the wind, and it would look festive."

"It seems someone has found the Christmas spirit," Harley said. "You weren't all that enthusiastic about decorating when Serena first suggested it."

"I was enthusiastic. I was just concerned about the cost and time commitment. But then you stepped up to help. And there's something about a rescue involving Santa that brings the magic of the season into play."

"Well, I'm happy the whole team is behind the project." Harley took a step back and looked at the building. "Maybe we need lights in the trees."

"That would look awesome, but I'm not sure the electrical system can handle many more lights than we already have."

"I guess I'll have to upgrade the electrical system before next year. I bought a generator for the house. Maybe something like that would work for tree lights."

"If you want to go to all that expense, I think it would look great."

Harley and I worked side by side until the shelter looked as if it might ignite from all the lights. I was just about to suggest we head inside for some hot cocoa when a man in a Chevy truck pulled up, got out, opened the back door, lifted an adorable yellow puppy who looked to be some sort of lab mix into his arms, and headed toward me.

"Do you work here?" he asked.

"Yes, I'm a volunteer."

He handed me the puppy, who I estimated to be four months old, turned, and walked back to his truck.

"Wait," I called after him. When he didn't stop, I thrust the puppy into Harley's arms and took off at a jog. "Are you surrendering this puppy?"

The man opened the driver's side door to his truck. "I am."

"Why?"

He glared at me with angry eyes. "I don't want or need a dog."

"So why did you get one?"

"I didn't. My mother wasn't happy that I decided to live all alone in this godforsaken wilderness, so she decided to remedy the situation by giving me a forty-pound pooping and chewing machine."

I put my hand out to stop him from leaving before I could have my say. "Puppies chew and poop in the most inopportune places, but with a little training…"

He slipped into the truck. "I'm not interested."

"Do you live here in town?" I wondered.

He shook his head. "About an hour north of here. Now, if you don't mind…"

I stood back. He closed his door and drove away.

I stamped down my anger. Some people! Of course I was glad the man had dropped the puppy off with us and not simply abandoned it, as some folks were apt to do. I watched the truck pull onto the highway and out of sight, then turned around and headed to where the pup was slathering doggy kisses all over Harley's face. I laughed. "He likes you."

"Maybe, but that doesn't mean I have room in my life for a dog."

Feigning innocence, I replied, "Did I say I thought you'd be a good match for this little cutie?"

"No, but I know you, and I've seen you work your magic on others. First, you point out how cute the little guy is, and then you casually mention how much the pup likes me. Once I admit to that, in theory at least, you segue into a comment about it being the holidays and the shelter being overcrowded, and say how nice it would be if the pup had a home for Christmas. While I attempt to extract myself from the situation by pointing out all the very real reasons a puppy wouldn't work for me, eventually, I find myself seduced by your sweet smile and big brown eyes, and before I realize what's happened, this energetic little chewing machine is entrenched in my house, happily eating my sofa, as I try to figure out how on earth you talked me into bringing him home in the first place."

I laughed. "Very good. That's exactly what I'd planned. So how about it? Just for a few days, until I can find someone to foster him."

"I thought the whole reason you wanted to open this shelter was to house the local animals that have been abandoned."

"It is," I replied. "And you know how much I and everyone value your contribution. But this little guy is just a baby. He needs training and attention. He would be better off in a home."

Harley hesitated.

"But if you're too busy, I guess I can ask Wyatt, or maybe Landon. Neither would be as good with him as you, but beggars can't be choosers." I sighed in such a way as to indicate the situation was a lot direr than it was.

He let out a long breath. "Okay, fine. But just for a few days. I can't have a dog on a permanent basis. I travel all the time. It wouldn't be practical."

"I know. And a few days will help a lot." I stood on tiptoe and kissed Harley on the cheek. "Let's go inside. I'll see if I can find a collar and a leash, and then we'll head to the pet store."

"Pet store?"

"The pup is going to need things. Food. A bed. Some toys and grooming supplies. You know, all the standard stuff. Oh, and a name. We can't keep calling him *the pup*."

"I'm not naming him."

I shrugged. "Okay, I will. How about Rudolph?"

Harley raised a brow. "Rudolph?"

"It's almost Christmas, and the man did say he lived up north. Rudolph seems like an appropriate name for a Christmas puppy from up north."

Harley held out the pup and took a closer look. "He's going to be a big dog. And I can already tell he's smart. He needs a name with some dignity. How about Brando?"

I smiled. It looked like Brando had found a new daddy, whether Harley knew it or not.

Chapter 3

Harley, Brando, and I had just returned from the pet store when I got a call from Jake, letting me know we had another rescue. It was going to be dark in a few hours, so time was of the essence. I quickly went over a few things with Harley, including the use of the large dog crate we'd purchased and the basic theory behind training a smart and energetic puppy, and headed out after promising to check back in with him that evening. Jake had indicated the man we were going to be looking for was a member of fellow S&R member Dani Mathew's heli-skiing party, and with the depth of the snow on the mountain, the dogs wouldn't be utilized for this rescue. I drove to the airport, where I found Jake, Wyatt, Landon, and Houston all waiting for Dani to arrive.

"What's the situation?" I asked, after greeting everyone.

"Dani called me just before I called you. She informed me that she had taken six men up the mountain for the ski trip, but only five showed up at the rendezvous point. It's starting to snow up there, so time is of the essence if we're going to have a chance of finding the sixth skier alive. She's on her way back with the five men. Wyatt, Landon, and I will go back up with Dani. Harmony can head to the inn with Houston and the men." Jake looked at me. "It will be important to make a connection. Get a photo. Talk to the five. Do whatever you can to get what we need."

I nodded. "I'll try."

"The men were dressed for a day on the mountain, which will buy us some time," Jake added. "But with the early sunset, we don't have a lot of daylight left. We need to know where to search."

I looked up as the chopper came into view. It looked so small against the dark and brooding sky. I watched as it got closer, stirring the air around us. I imagined the wind up on the mountain was fierce.

After Jake and the others left, Houston and I accompanied the five men to the inn. When Dani had dropped them off, she'd given Houston a heads-up that something seemed strange to her. Houston wanted to speak to the men individually, but first, he wanted me to have a chance to connect with the one who was missing, so he sent the others into the kitchen for coffee and a snack while I pulled up the photo Dani had taken of the whole group before they headed down the mountain, and focused on the thin man with dark hair and a narrow face.

I took a deep breath and closed my eyes. All the men looked happy as they posed for the photo. They were laughing, with their arms around one another before preparing their descent. It took an expert skier to handle the mountain, which had steep drop-offs as well as gently curving runs established by others who'd tackled it in the days since the last heavy snow.

I tried to bring an image of the man into my mind. I knew his name was Piney Portman, and that he was an attorney and a decent skier. Jake had established those facts when he first spoke to Dani. I also knew all the men in the group had been childhood friends who vacationed together on a fairly regular basis. I opened my eyes and looked at the photo again. I wasn't getting anything. It seemed by now Portman must be aware he was in a dangerous situation. I assumed he'd be frightened. I was usually able to pick up on the frightened. Unless he was already dead; then I wouldn't be able to make a connection at all. I was about to give up and go into the kitchen to question the men when I had a brief flash. I looked around the room. The flash wasn't a connection to the man we were hoping to rescue but to someone else in the inn. My ability to connect with individuals I wasn't tasked to find was a new development I'd yet learned to channel. As it had been in the past, the image in my mind was nothing more than a flash that was gone almost before it appeared.

I picked up my radio, then took it on to the front porch, where I wouldn't be overheard. "Harmony to Dani."

"Go for Dani," she responded from the radio in her chopper.

"I wasn't able to connect with the victim. I think he's dead. I had a flash, like the flash of a memory I picked up from Zane Hudson." I referred to the man who'd killed several people, including a member of our team in October.

"What did you see?" Dani asked.

"Portman is lying on a ridge." I paused, trying to remember. "I'm pretty sure it's the ridge that's off to the left after you come out of Snake Canyon."

"I'll let the others know to look there," Dani said. "You said you picked up a memory. Does that mean one of the men in the ski party knows what became of his friend?"

"I think that's what it means. This ability to pick up images from individuals other than the victim is new and I haven't figured it all out yet, but it seems as if the memory I piggybacked on to must have been from one of the others who were with him. I need to figure out which friend it came from."

I signed off with Dani and went inside, then pulled Houston aside. I explained what had occurred and he decided to speak to each man individually, starting with Drake Weston, a twenty-eight-year-old real estate developer. Houston asked me to sit in to observe, hoping I'd be able to figure out which friend's memory I'd connected with.

Drake informed Houston he'd first met Anton Willowby, Lucas Smith, Reggie Slater, Colin Barker, and Piney Portman when they were on the same Little League team in the first grade. They'd formed a bond when their team went undefeated, which earned them a spot in the regional championships. The boys had stayed together as a team in the years that followed, and remained close friends throughout grade school and into high school. According to Drake, they were as close as brothers could be, spending a lot of time in one another's company. They made a point of spending long weekends together three or four times a year, as well as longer trips at least annually.

Houston asked if all of them had always gotten along with one another. After a bit of prodding, Drake admitted there'd been tension between some of them from time to time, but it always blew over. Houston asked for an example of a time when tension occurred, and Drake responded that the most recent tension was during the trip to the lake house they'd rented the previous summer, when Piney and Anton both expressed interest in the woman who'd rented the cabin next door. Drake was pretty sure they'd made up, with no lingering resentments between them. Other women had come between the men from time to time, but Drake had seen that lessening as the men began to enter into long-term relationships. Lucas and Reggie had become engaged, and their fiancées were both with them on this trip. Houston asked where the women were today; apparently, they'd gone into Fairbanks on a shopping excursion. Although neither he nor Anton had brought their girlfriends with them on this trip, the only two not currently involved in serious relationships were Piney and Colin, who never seemed to date.

Drake provided an overview of the other men and their reason for being in Rescue, and then Houston asked him what had happened on the mountain that day.

He frowned before answering. "I'm not really sure. It was windier than any of us anticipated, and after landing and getting an idea of how the weather actually was, the helicopter pilot suggested we might want to reschedule. I was neutral, but Reggie was adamant that we ski down as we'd planned, and Anton agreed with him. Lucas made a few good points about the superior condition of the snow, and most of the guys agreed the fresh powder was too good to pass up, although Piney voiced his concern about the visibility and Colin pointed out that the wind was coming from behind the mountain, which meant once we dropped down into the little valley, we should be protected from the worst of it. In the end, we decided to go for it. The pilot agreed to wait for us about halfway down the mountain. She told us we could decide to either continue on or catch a ride at that point."

"And it was at that point you realized Mr. Portman was missing?" Houston asked.

Drake nodded. "In the beginning we were all together, but some of us are faster skiers than the others, so by the time we made it to the rendezvous point, we were pretty spread out. When I arrived, Lucas and Anton were already there. Colin was right behind me, and I assumed Piney and Reggie were somewhere just behind him. Reggie showed up maybe fifteen minutes after Colin, but Piney never showed. Colin insisted Piney was in the first group, with Lucas and Anton, and Lucas and Anton said they hadn't seen him since we all took off at the top."

"What did you do when Piney didn't show?" Houston asked.

Drake's expression became guarded. "We tried to figure out what might have happened to him. First we talked about who had seen what, then we looked around. We were limited in what we could do with all the snow. It wasn't like we could hike back up the mountain. Colin suggested we take the chopper back to the top and try to find Piney as we skied down a second time, but the pilot, suggested we come here and let the professionals take over. By then everyone was cold and scared. I wasn't sure what was best, but I decided to agree to the pilot's plan and the others went along with it too."

"So you really have no idea if Piney was in front of or behind you once everyone began to scatter?" I verified.

He shook his head. "The visibility was bad up on the mountain, despite it not being all that windy when we left Rescue. I know we should have listened to the pilot when she warned us it was risky to continue. I thought Piney was in front of me, but I can't be sure. I was focused on watching my own GPS coordinates so I didn't end up lost and wasn't paying as much attention to the others as I should have been."

Houston asked Drake a few more questions and then sent him to the kitchen while we spoke to Lucas Smith. Lucas was a commercial contractor and developer who was engaged to Miranda Colton, one of the two women who'd come on the trip.

Lucas provided a set up similar to that provided by Drake. Six good buddies had gotten together for a ski week in Alaska. Houston asked Lucas about his recollections of the events of the day, and he shared that after they made the decision to head down the mountain, he put his head down and never looked back. He was the first one to arrive at the meeting place chosen by Dani. He also said she could verify that, which Houston shared that he planned to confirm but had no reason to doubt. Lucas said Piney was a better than average skier; not quite as good as he was, but better than most. If it turned out Piney had simply fallen or gone off course, Lucas would be very much surprised, though with the sketchy conditions, it was possible he met with an obstacle he wasn't able to avoid.

Anton Willowby sat down with us next. Like the others, he told us Reggie was the one who'd called him with the idea of the trip. Anton hadn't really wanted to go at first, but he felt it made sense from a business perspective, so he agreed. When Houston asked what he meant by that, Anton said the men had all gone into fields that complemented one another, and at times two or more of them were working together on projects. Houston asked Anton to elaborate, and he explained he was an accountant, Drake a real estate developer, Lucas a commercial contractor, Reggie an investment banker, Colin a commercial real estate agent, and Piney a business attorney.

It was during our interview with the fourth man, Reggie Slater, that Jake called to let Houston know they'd found Piney Portman exactly where I'd said he would be. Unfortunately, as I suspected, he was already dead. Not only that, all indications were that he might have been murdered. It looked like our missing persons investigation had just turned into a murder investigation.

******

After Houston had interviewed all five of the men, he excused me to head to Neverland for the debriefing, while he stayed behind to do some additional digging.

"If Piney Portman was murdered, as the scene of his death suggests, he has to have been killed by one of the five other men in the ski party," Dani insisted.

"Not only did Harmony get a peek at a memory of someone at the inn, I didn't see anyone else up on the mountain."

"Fill me in on why you think he was murdered," said Sarge, former military and the cook at Neverland, who hadn't been in on this rescue.

"We found the body on a ledge a good hundred feet below where he had to have gone over," Landon provided. "He landed on some rocks and we knew for certain he couldn't have survived, but we won't be able to get a close look at the body until it's recovered. There was evidence of two sets of ski tracks on the bluff above, as well as signs of a struggle and blood in the snow in a few areas, like rock groupings, protected from the wind. That indicated, to Jake and me, that Portman was involved in an altercation before going over the ledge. Until the storm lets up and it's safe to retrieve the body, there isn't a lot more that can be said one way or another."

"When do you think you'll be able to get the body?" I asked Dani.

"The wind is supposed to let up overnight. I should be able to land on the ledge tomorrow."

"Wyatt and I will head out at first light with Dani," Jake said. "If she can land anywhere near the body, we should be able to bring him in. Maybe there will be evidence on the body to indicate what might have occurred."

"Has Houston told the other members of the ski party you suspect foul play?" Sarge asked.

I shook my head. "No. He conducted the interviews in such a way as to suggest he was only trying to determine how an accident might have occurred, and you hadn't found the body until he'd spoken with most of them. The group is planning to be here until the twenty-third, which should give him time to sort everything out."

"What about motive?" Jake's girlfriend and team member Dr. Jordan Fairchild asked.

Everyone turned to me. "I'm not sure. All five claimed they were a close-knit group who'd been best friends since first grade. Several of them mentioned occasional tension between some of them from time to time, but no one made it out to sound as if it was the kind of thing that destroys relationships. They worked together at times, and all of them agreed to come on this trip. It would seem they'd mended fences and whatever went on in the past was resolved. Still, I was picking something up. And not from just one of them. They all seemed to be holding something back." I frowned. "I'll try to talk to them again after we retrieve the body. Maybe someone will let something slip. Everyone had his guard up big-time today."

"The women who are traveling with them might be able to provide some insight as well," Jordan pointed out.

"Houston and I discussed that. They hadn't returned to the inn before I left to come over here, but I know he planned to speak to them."

"I wonder why the men didn't stay together," Jordan said. "I mean, with the weather conditions, I'd think they'd realize there was safety in numbers."

I shifted in my chair so the fire in the stone fireplace could warm my other side. "Houston asked them that. They all said they had differing skill levels, and the ones who were faster didn't want to wait for the ones who were slower, so they agreed to meet up at the helicopter."

"Do we know in what order they arrived at the helicopter?" Sarge asked.

"Lucas Smith was first, followed by Anton Willowby. Shortly after that, Reggie Slater showed up, followed by Colin Barker and Drake Weston, who came in so close together, I didn't notice which came in first," Dani answered.

"And was Piney Portman fast or slow?" Jordan asked.

"That's the odd thing. The men in the front of the pack swear he was behind them, and those at the back swear he was in front of them. We couldn't find two of the five who agreed on this detail," I answered. "No one claims to have seen Portman after they took off from the top, but it seems obvious to me that if he was killed, one of the five killed him."

"It does seem as if one of the five must be the killer if Piney was murdered." Jake looked at me. "Are you sure the flash of memory you experienced was from someone in the inn?"

I nodded. "Yes, I think so. To be honest I can't be a hundred percent certain, but if I had to guess whose memory I hijacked, I would say the person who held the memory was in close proximity."

"Were there any other guests in the inn other than the five men who went on the ski trip?" Jake asked.

"Yes. Houston spoke to Mary about the guests. In addition to the six men on the ski trip and the two women who accompanied them, Nick Clauston and his daughter and her husband are still at the inn, although they planned to leave after what happened this morning. Mary said there were four other guests, including a visiting businessman from Germany named Deidrick Eckhart, who Mary pointed out as the gray haired man reading in the front parlor, a skier who had gone out earlier in the day named Walter Sandman, who Mary described as early thirties with light hair, and a couple named Fred and Victoria Pendleton, a retired history professor and his wife from Connecticut."

"Is it possible any of them were on the mountain when Piney was killed?" Jake asked.

"I suppose it's possible the skier went up the mountain with another heli-skiing tour. As far as I know, he wasn't in the inn when Houston and I were there. We didn't verify his whereabouts, but maybe." I looked around. "I think it's probably a waste of time to look for other suspects. My gut tells me one of the five men is the killer."

Chapter 4

It was completely dark when I got home. My little cabin looked cold and forlorn after all the lights in town. With the memories stirred up by the decorations at the inn, I'd momentarily considered buying some lights, and maybe a few small things to replace the ones I'd lost, but money was tight as usual, and it seemed smarter to stock up on food for me and my animals. Supplies would get even thinner as the winter wore on, so spending money on frivolous things really didn't make sense at all.

Grabbing a flashlight and my rifle, I headed out into the darkness to walk the dogs. Yukon took a position in the front of the pack, with my wolf hybrid Denali and my husky mix Shia, while my two retired sled dogs, Juno and Kodi, settled into the middle. I walked slowly so my three-legged dog, Lucky, could keep up on the trail I'd packed down with my snowmobile, and Honey, my retriever, trotted along right next to him.

I preferred to walk the dogs when it was light, but with so few hours of daylight now, walking in the dark was inevitable. This presented a certain level of danger; the area I could see with my flashlight was severely limited. I'd been seeing cougar prints in the snow the last few days, so I planned a short walk tonight, rather than going all the way out to the lake, which I might have done during daylight hours.

I had just called the dogs back in anticipation of turning around when I heard barking from the front of the pack. "Denali, Yukon, come," I shouted into the darkness.

After a brief pause, Yukon returned, but Denali was still missing. He tended to have a mind of his own, but I'd heard the echoes of the wolves who lived nearby earlier. Hopefully, Denali wouldn't engage. I whistled loudly, then called his name again. After a couple of minutes he came to where the other dogs and I were waiting. He was wagging his tail and looked happy as could be, so I guessed he must have discovered a rabbit or squirrel, not a predator or intruder.

"You need to stay with me," I scolded the large dog. "I can't be searching in the dark for you if you get it in your head to run off."

Denali wagged his tail, then trotted back toward the house. There was only so much I could do to train the stubborn dog, and most of the time when he disobeyed it was for a good reason.

When I returned to the house I found a large box on the front porch. It was wrapped in green paper with a brown piece of string for ribbon. I picked it up, looking for a tag, but there wasn't one. Curious, I looked around, in search of fresh footprints. There were so many dog prints, it was hard to make out one print from another, but it looked as if whoever had dropped off the package had both arrived and left via the forest. Who would be walking around on a night like this? The image of Santa flashed into my mind for the tenth time that day. I shrugged and smiled, then took the box inside and set it on the dining table. I couldn't imagine who would leave a gift on my doorstep. It was still ten days until Christmas, so a bit early for gifts anyway. Besides, no one I knew would leave an anonymous gift. Jake and I exchanged gifts every Christmas and the others from the search-and-rescue team usually had a dinner on Christmas Eve at which we exchanged small tokens. Harley had given me a gift last year, but he'd waited until Christmas Eve. Chloe and I usually exchanged gifts, but we normally did it during a meal a day or two before the actual holiday. I shook the box and heard something rattling, but that wasn't much of a clue to what might be inside.

Should I open it? Should I wait? Making a quick decision, I went into the kitchen for my scissors. I had to dig through my junk drawer to find them and was just returning to the box when Denali started to growl.

"What is it? Do you hear something?"

Denali ran to the front door and began to bark. Yukon followed immediately. No one had knocked and I hadn't seen a light from a vehicle, so I picked up my rifle and headed to the main entry. I peered out the window next to the door but didn't see anything. I slowly opened the door and gasped. On the porch was a box and inside it were five kittens. "You poor things," I said aloud as I picked up the box and brought it inside. "I wonder why you weren't dropped off at the shelter."

The shelter was closed to drop-offs at this time of night, so I supposed whoever had left the kittens hadn't wanted to wait. I made sure they were uninjured, then made up bowls of soft food mixed with the milk replacement I kept on hand and set them on the kitchen floor. The kittens didn't seem all that hungry, but being thrust into a strange house with seven dogs and four cats was probably a bit intimidating. I managed to get a few bites into each one before changing my plan of attack. Grabbing a heated pet bed from my supply closet, I went into my guest room and set up a little nest for the kittens, then set up a cat box and an eating area where I could leave some food. I settled the kittens with a soft blanket in an area I could block off with furniture. With the lights turned down low, I left them alone so they could take some time to settle in. I figured I'd check on them in an hour. Hopefully, they wouldn't be so frightened once they had a chance to adjust and I could get more food in them. I could take them to the shelter tomorrow, but they were awfully tiny. It might be best to keep them here with me until they were old enough to be adopted.

I returned to the main living area, where my cats and dogs were waiting for their own meals. I fed everyone, cleaned cat boxes, and then went out to the barn to see to the rabbits and Homer. He couldn't see me, but he seemed to enjoy my presence, so I chatted to him about my day as I cleaned his stall. After my old barn had burned down, my neighbors had gotten together to build a brand-new and far superior one. I was still out my Christmas decorations, as well as the other things I'd stored in the old barn, but I was so grateful for a safe, warm, dry place to house Homer and the rabbits, I didn't mind.

When I returned to the extra bedroom an hour later to check on the kittens, I found the door cracked open. Strange; I was sure I'd pulled it closed behind me. Maybe it hadn't clicked. I opened the door a bit more and tiptoed inside to find my mama dog, Honey, curled up on the heated pad with all five kittens tucked in tight between her legs. My heart filled with warmth as I took in the sight before me. I'd thought I'd had a good plan, but Honey's worked just as well.

When I'd found Honey last Christmas, she'd been pregnant herself. She'd been a wonderful mother to her own pups, nurturing every one until it was time for them to go to wonderful forever homes. Since she'd been with me, she'd fostered several of the babies who'd entered my life, including a bear cub the night his mother was shot.

I supposed that all the animals in my menagerie seemed to have come to me for some purpose. Denali was my protector, Yukon my search-and-rescue partner, Shia was the funny one, and Lucky was the one who gave me hope. Each animal was loved and appreciated for their own personality and contribution to my life. I supposed Honey's purpose was clearly to provide comfort and to nurture the babies I picked up along the way. Making a quick decision, I transferred both Honey and the kittens to the larger dog bed in my bedroom. That was where I should have put the kittens in the first place, but I'd thought they might be nervous sharing space with the five dogs who slept with me. While they'd been skittish at first, with

Honey to look out for them, they'd probably be content to hang out with the rest of us.

Tossing another log on the fire, I snuggled onto the sofa and used the remote to turn on the TV. I wasn't a huge television watcher, but there was a Christmas romance movie set on a ranch in Montana I wanted to see. If history served as a predictor, I'd watch it until I fell asleep about halfway through. The setting was beautiful, which added to my enjoyment. The first commercials had come on when my phone rang.

"I thought you were going to come by to check on Brando after the rescue," Harley said.

I had totally forgotten about my promise. "I'm sorry," I answered. "I did say I would. I only just got home a little while ago. By the time I walked the dogs, fed everyone, and cleaned stalls and cat boxes, it was late. But I still should have called. I really am sorry."

Harley let out a breath. "That's okay. It sounds as if you were busy."

"How's the pup doing?"

Harley hesitated. "He's okay. He ate one of my slippers. It was Italian leather, so it made for an expensive chew toy, but otherwise he seems to have settled in. He sure has a lot of energy. After I fed him and put him to sleep, I felt like I'd been involved in hand-to-hand combat."

I grinned. "Puppies do tend to be high on energy. Especially lab puppies. Have you tried the crate we picked up at the pet store?"

"He's sleeping in it right now. I played with him until we were both on the verge of exhaustion, then I put him in the crate with a heated blanket and some toys. I'm hoping he'll sleep through the night. Do you think he will?"

"He should. And if he wakes up, he won't be able to get out of the crate, so he should be fine. You'll want to take him outside immediately after you let him out of the crate in the morning. And I mean immediately. Don't stop to make coffee or turn on the television or anything."

"Got it. Take the puppy out to pee first, have coffee second. I still don't know how you talked me into this."

I couldn't help but remember his comment about my sweet smile and big brown eyes. "I guess I just have a knack for persuasion."

"I'd say you're the queen of persuasion. If anyone would have told me yesterday that I'd be talked into babysitting a puppy, even for a few days, I would have said they were nuts."

"You're doing a good thing."

"I know. And he's pretty cute, even if he runs around with his mouth open so he won't have to stop when he finds the next thing he wants to chew up."

"It'll get better. I promise. Tomorrow we'll go over correcting and replacing. Once you get the hang of that, his training will move quickly."

"I hope so. I'd hate it if he ate the wrong thing and it made him sick."

"Some puppy proofing of your house wouldn't be a bad idea. An even better idea is to make him stay in his crate when you aren't able to keep an eye on him. It's a big crate and he has a lot of toys to keep him occupied. He'll be fine in it for short periods of time."

"He looks at me like I'm some kind of traitor when I put him in it."

"After a while he'll actually learn to like it. You'll see."

"You sound like I'm going to have this dog for more than a few days," Harley said, a tone of accusation in his voice.

"It might be hard to place him before Christmas," I responded. "But shortly after. I promise."

Harley sighed. "Oh, all right. It might be nice to have someone to wake up to on Christmas morning."

I was willing to bet there were a lot of someones who'd be willing to wake up next to Harley if he asked. Before I got to know him, I'd let the tabloids convince me he woke up to a different someone pretty much every morning.

"By the way," Harley said, "I meant to ask if you still wanted to go to the Christmas festival tomorrow."

"I'd like to."

"Do you think Brando will be okay?"

I considered that. "I think so. For a few hours. How about if I come over in the morning and spend some time working on his training? That usually tires puppies out. When he's good and tuckered out, we can put him in his crate and head into town for a few hours."

"That sounds great. Why don't you text me in the morning to let me know when you'll be here?"

"I'll need to walk the dogs and feed the clan, which has grown by five kittens as of this evening."

"Five kittens?"

"Someone left them in a box on my doorstep. They're pretty small, but they look healthy, and Honey has taken over the nurturing part of their care. I thought about taking them to the shelter tomorrow, but I think I'll just keep them here until they're old enough to go to forever homes."

"Do any of the pets you have there ever end up in the shelter?" Harley asked.

I laughed. "A few."

Actually a lot, but Harley knew that because he was at the facility almost as much as I was when he was in town. I chatted with him for a few more minutes, then hung up.

I knew Jake planned to go up the mountain with Dani in the morning to retrieve Piney Portman's body. He might need to call a meeting of the search-and-rescue team after that. I should call him to ask about his plans. Neverland was closed on Sundays, so he usually took the time to watch football or go skiing, but if Portman really had been murdered, the entire search-and-rescue team might be pulled into the investigation. Not that Houston wasn't a great cop. He was. But because the two men he'd inherited when he took the job of police chief were somewhat lazy and unenthusiastic, so when it came to really investigating a case, he was on his own. I'd already helped him out with several pretty complex cases. I knew he valued my input and wouldn't be surprised if he asked for it again. It was really a win-win situation because working with Houston had turned out to be one of the most satisfying things I'd done recently. And not just working with him on the murder cases that had landed on his desk, but as he developed his own S&R dog. Like Yukon, Kojak had been a stray, but also like him, Kojak seemed to have a lot of natural talent and was making progress at an amazing rate. I imagined our two-dog team would be a three-dog team before the summer rescue season.

Chapter 5

Sunday, December 16

It was pitch black when I awoke the next morning. I groaned as I rolled out of bed, grabbed a heavy sweatshirt and a pair of knee-high slippers, and padded into the main living area of the cabin. I turned on the coffeemaker, then went to find Honey and the kittens, who were all missing from the dog bed. After a bit of searching, I found them sleeping under my bed. I called to Honey and the kittens followed.

"Hey there, sweetie," I said, picking up one of the kittens. It might have been my sleep-deprived brain at work, but darn it if the kitten didn't look fluffier. Perhaps Honey had cleaned her up. She certainly looked perkier. I scratched her under her chin as I cuddled her to my chest. She actually began to purr. Calling Honey and the other four kittens to follow, I went back out into the living area. I set the kitten down near a saucer of milk replacement, then arranged bowls for the others. I pulled on my heavy boots and a jacket, grabbing my rifle, and took the dogs out for a quick bathroom break.

When I returned, I fed the dogs and cats, then settled in with my first cup of coffee of the day. Noticing the box, still sitting wrapped on my dining table, I grabbed the scissors and cut the string. I peeled back the paper and opened the lid to find several strings of brand-new lights. Outdoor lights. The very lights I'd been thinking I wished I had for the cabin. Had someone read my mind?

I reached into the box and pulled out the lights. Who on earth even knew I needed lights? Landon? We'd discussed them the day before, but I couldn't see him running out and buying an anonymous gift. Jake might have realized my Christmas decorations would have been destroyed in the fire. Or perhaps Chloe? My money was on her, although there was no way she'd tromp through the woods to drop the box off anonymously. Still, I'd ask her when I went into town. I was grateful to whoever left the lights. The more I thought about it, the more I realized that lights on the cabin would go a long way toward bringing the spirit of the holiday into my life.

As I finished my first cup of coffee, I received a text from Harley, asking if I still planned to come by for a training session. I told him I did and asked if he had any food in his house. He said he did and offered to make me breakfast. If I jumped into the shower, I could be at his house in an hour.

When I arrived at Harley's, I was greeted by a bundle of fur with a sock in his mouth. I raised an eye at Harley who, upon noticing the sock, tried to grab it, which only made the pup run. After watching the battle of wits between man and dog for a solid minute, I called a halt to things by clapping my hands loudly to get the attention of both dog and man. "Don't chase him," I cautioned Harley. "He wants you to chase him."

"He's eating my sock."

"Italian cotton?" I chuckled.

Harley smiled. "No. Just regular cotton."

I pulled a treat out of my pocket, then called the pup over. He immediately ran toward me, skidding on the floor, and sliding into my legs. "Good dog, Brando."

The dog jumped up, shaking his head as if to shake the stars from his eyes, then jumped up onto my leg. I took a step forward, which made him fall backward. The pup looked confused, but I'd gotten his attention. He stood up again and I took control, telling him to sit. He must have been taught that by his previous owner because he plopped his butt on the floor. I put out my hand and asked for the sock. He was reluctant to give it to me, but eventually, he dropped it at my feet. I praised him and gave him a treat. "Has he been out?"

"I took him just before you got here."

"Okay. Let's eat first and work on the training after."

"First, while it's still dark, I want to show you the lights I set up in the back." Harley took my hand and led me from the entry and down the hallway toward the back of the house. Opening the door off the laundry room, he stepped out and I followed. All I could do was gasp. It looked as if he'd hung every light in town in the back of his admittedly huge estate. "Wow."

"It's really something, isn't it?" Harley grinned as I stepped out onto the covered patio, which looked like a fairyland.

I nodded slowly. "I would say that's an understatement. Now I understand why you had to buy a generator to run the lights."

Harley flipped a switch, and mechanical bears began to move across the snow. "I guess it's a bit much, but I haven't been anywhere that felt even remotely like home for Christmas for a very long time. I guess I got carried away when I started ordering stuff, but I sure had fun putting everything up." Harley grabbed my hand. "Come on. I can't wait to show you the living room."

After seeing the outside of the house, I was almost afraid to see what he'd done to the inside, which was why I was pleasantly surprised to find a more toned-down but equally spectacular interior design. The huge tree rose two stories into the air and was decorated to complement the real fir garland on the mantel and stair railing. "Wow, it's beautiful. It looks like you used a designer."

"I did," Harley admitted. "Sort of. My sister Polly came over and helped me with the interior. I think she was shocked enough by what I'd done to the outside that she realized I'd need a gentler hand in here."

"Well, it looks spectacular."

"Thanks. Let's go to the kitchen. I have a fire going in the fireplace and a breakfast casserole in the oven."

"A casserole? You can cook?"

"I don't know how to make many things, but the few things I can are pretty darn good. After you've had my eggs Benedict casserole, you'll never look at breakfast the same way again."

No, I decided. I was sure I wouldn't.

******

We ate the most delicious meal I think I'd ever eaten, then worked with Brando for a solid hour, put him down for a nap, and headed to town and the Winter Wonderland Christmas Celebration. It was as loud and crowded when we arrived as it had been the day before. Harley didn't seem to mind the chaos. In fact, I thought he was enjoying it quite a lot. He bought a bunch of items from the bake sale that he planned to drop off for the shelter volunteers and made the rounds to all the booths selling Christmas trinkets, buying things from some and stopping to chat with everyone.

"Oh look, a baseball toss," he said as we approached the area set aside for games. "Hold my stuff and I'll win you a stuffed moose."

"You have to knock all the bottles down on the first throw to get a home run, and you need three home runs in a row to win a stuffed moose. I think that's pretty hard to do."

"O ye, of little faith." Harley gave the man five dollars, then stood back. He narrowed his gaze, turned to his side, then threw the ball as hard as he could.

"Oh my gosh, you did it." I clapped after all the bottles went crashing down.

"One down and just two to go." Harley winked at me.

I don't know why I'd doubted that an action superstar like Harley Medford would be able to knock down ten bottles with one throw three times in a row, but as he'd indicated he would, he managed to do so and made it look effortless. I noticed that when the man handed him the moose, Harley slipped a hundred-dollar bill into the cashbox. The moose probably cost less than twenty bucks, but I guess he wanted to make sure the fund-raiser raised a lot of funds.

"What now?" Harley asked as he handed me the giant stuffed animal.

I looked around the room. It was hot and crowded and I really would prefer to leave if Harley was finished with what he wanted to do. I was just about to suggest as much when I noticed two of the men from the ski group standing near the line to the beer garden with two very beautiful women.

"See the men with the two dark-haired women in line for the beer garden?" I asked Harley.

"Yeah. I see them."

"Their names are Lucas Smith and Reggie Slater. They were on the heli-skiing trip yesterday. The women must be their fiancées. They were in Fairbanks when the rescue occurred so I didn't meet them."

"Do you want to talk to them?" Harley asked.

"Actually, I do."

Harley looked around the room. "Let's take this stuff out to the truck and then come back. You can introduce me to the guys, which should open the door for them to introduce you to the women."

We stashed the moose he'd won and the things he'd purchased in the back seat and then went back inside. I wasn't sure what I was expecting; certainly not that Lucas and Reggie's fiancées would look like supermodels. I wondered what they were doing here at this local event. Based on appearances alone, I would have pegged them to be the champagne and caviar sort, not the type to enjoy beer and nachos to the sound of kiddie carols.

"Lucas, Reggie. How nice to see you," I said.

They both looked surprised and not all that happy to see me. Until they noticed who I was with.

"You're Harley Medford," Reggie gushed.

"The last time I checked." Harley laughed.

I made the introductions. "Lucas Smith, Reggie Slater, this is Harley Medford, which I guess you already figured out."

Harley held out his hand. "Nice to meet you."

"Anabelle Chamberlin," the woman who was with Reggie introduced herself. "What on earth is a superstar like Harley Medford doing at this Podunk affair?"

"I live in Rescue and I'm here to support the local cause," Harley answered.

"I think that's really nice," the woman with Lucas said. "Miranda Colton." She took Harley's hand.

"You live in Rescue?" Lucas asked, furrowing his brow so tightly, it appeared he had a crater in his forehead. "Why?"

Harley shrugged. "I grew up here. Besides, I like the slow, steady way of life. It's so different from Los Angeles."

"I'm sure that much is true," Lucas replied.

"Can we buy you a beer?" Reggie asked.

Harley looked at me. "I wouldn't mind a beer," I answered, jumping on the opening I needed. "Why don't you wait in line with the guys, Harley, and Miranda, Anabelle, and I will find a table."

I set off across the room with the two women.

"I can't believe you're friends with Harley Medford," Miranda said as we slid into three of the chairs at a table for six. "He is now and has always been my number-one celebrity crush."

"He is quite delicious to look at," Anabelle agreed. "I don't know how you can keep yourself from ripping his clothes off."

Miranda gasped, but I just smiled and raised a brow. "Who said I stopped myself from doing just that?"

Anabelle appeared to be impressed, but Miranda inhaled in what could only be described as total shock and disbelief. "Oh my God, Harley Medford is your boyfriend?"

I laughed. "No. He isn't my boyfriend. Exactly." I decided to let that dangle. "So, I understand you two are engaged to Lucas and Reggie." I realized if I wanted to find out anything from them, I needed to do my prying before the men joined us.

"Anabelle and Reggie have been engaged for a year and Lucas and I for four months," Miranda answered.

"And the four of you are friends?" I asked. "I mean, outside of this ski trip."

"Sure," Miranda answered. "Anabelle and I have been friends for a long time. She introduced me to Lucas after she and Reggie got serious about their relationship."

"And the others?" I asked.

"The guys have been friends for a long time," Anabelle said. "Tell me some more about Harley. Is he good in bed? I bet he's great in bed."

Miranda gasped and I almost choked on my gum. I suspected my little white lie about Harley was going to get me into trouble if I didn't come clean. I was just about to do that when the guys appeared and the conversation naturally segued to movies Harley had starred in. I'd hoped to get more out of Miranda and Anabelle about what had happened the previous day, but the guys had been too quick, my opportunity evaporating.

By the time everyone had finished their beer I'd learned very little other than that Drake and Reggie, who'd been working together, had hoped to use the time in Alaska to convince Lucas to get on board with their project. I had a feeling that the business deals they were involved in could be relevant, but I needed time to do some digging and to think about things. Harley must have picked up on my subtle clues suggesting I'd had enough because he made an excuse to leave the others.

It was freezing outside, but after the heat inside, the cooler air felt good. At least for a moment.

"Well, that was interesting," Harley said.

I'm not quite sure why, but I burst out laughing.

"Something's funny?" Harley asked.

I hugged Harley's arm to my chest as we headed across the parking lot. "Anabelle made a suggestion I'm sure was meant to shock me, but instead, it seemed too good an opportunity not to turn the tables on her, which resulted in a bit of a white lie."

"I see. Dare I ask?"

I started giggling again. "Probably not."

Harley lifted his mouth in a half grin. "I don't suppose her suggestion had to do with you ripping my clothes off?"

I groaned. "You heard that?"

Harley laughed. "I came over to ask if you preferred light or dark beer, but when I heard the conversation I figured it was safer to flip a coin than to interrupt."

I groaned again. "I'm sorry. Anabelle made a jab and I responded. I guess it was pretty out of line."

Harley put his arm around my shoulders. "Oh, I don't know. I think your response was perfect."

I looked up. "So you aren't mad?"

Harley smiled. "Not at all. Of all the women I've been rumored to have slept with that I haven't, I think you're my favorite."

Chapter 6

"Piney Portman was stabbed in the neck with the sharp tip of a ski pole before he went over the edge of the cliff and fell to the rocks below," Houston informed Jake, Landon, Sarge, and me later that afternoon. I'd stopped by the bar to talk to Jake, who'd been having a beer and watching a football game with Landon and Sarge. The bar wasn't open on Sundays, but Sarge lived in the little apartment upstairs, and Jake lived in the big house across the parking lot, so they often got together to watch sports on the big-screen television provided for patrons.

"So we just need to test the ski poles of everyone who went up the mountain to see which pole has blood on it," I said.

"In theory, yes," Houston confirmed. "But it's been twenty-four hours. My sense is that the killer took care of any evidence by now, if there was anything. Still, I have my men picking up all the poles for testing."

"If we can't find any physical evidence to tie the killer to Piney's death, you'll need to really dig into the possible motive," I said. "If one of Piney's friends killed him, which is what I'm thinking, it seems if you dig around enough, you'll come up with a reason."

Houston nodded. "I think you're probably right. With physical evidence so slim at this point, it's likely we'll need to build a case based on motive and opportunity." Houston looked at me. "Now that you've had a chance to think things over, do any of the five suspects stand out to you as more likely to be the killer than the others?"

I sat back in my chair, took a deep breath, and took a moment to think about Houston's question. "In my opinion," I began, "every one of the men you spoke to yesterday seemed to be lying about something. I don't know if they were all lying about the same thing, or if each one was lying about something different, or if the lies relate to the murder at all, but there was definitely a cover-up going on."

"I agree," Houston said. He rested his elbows on the table and leaned forward. "I caught a general feeling of caution among all of them. If none of them was responsible for killing Piney, and none of them had anything to hide, they would have been gung ho to find out who killed their friend, but I didn't pick up that vibe at all. What I picked up was caution and hesitation. In some cases, it almost felt as if the answers they gave me had been thought out beforehand, possibly even rehearsed."

"Landon, Sarge, and I weren't involved in the interviews yesterday, so do you mind going over an abbreviated form of each one's statement?" Jake asked.

"Not at all," Houston answered. "I'd be happy to go over things, but we don't have much. I can say that Reggie Slater is an investment banker who's done quite well for himself. After speaking to the others, I had the feeling he's generally the one who plans the group trips, which have taken place all over the world. Anton Willowby said that last summer Reggie arranged a trip to Russia, and the winter before that they went skiing in Switzerland and hiking in Central America. Colin Barker, who's a commercial real estate agent, also mentioned trips to Turkey and China."

"They all must have deep pockets," I said.

"They seem to, with the exception of Piney. Based on what I found out from speaking to the men and scouring financial reports, it appears Piney, who has yet to make partner in his firm so doesn't make all that much, is still paying off his considerable school loans. In fact, based on the banking records I was able to find, it looks as if Reggie has been paying for Piney to come on these trips."

"What about Drake?" Jake asked.

"Drake is a real estate developer who seems to have done well for himself. He mentioned he and Reggie were working on a development together even before this trip. It sounded as if it was a big-ticket project that would require a lot of money up front, which is where Reggie came in. He seems to have both deep pockets and an impressive list of investors who've been linked to his projects internationally, so I plan to take a closer look at how this project might relate to whatever went on up on the mountain."

"What about Anton?" Landon asked. "He hasn't been discussed as much as the others. You said he was an accountant. It seems to me that if money is at the root of whatever happened, he'd be right in the middle of things."

Houston leaned back in his chair and stretched out his long legs. "Anton was very quiet and reserved when we spoke. He answered my questions as briefly as possible at times even limiting himself to yes and no answers, and he didn't volunteer a single thing. Based on what I got from the others, Anton is a good skier. Maybe the best in the group. I'm not saying he was the one who killed Piney, but if his ability on the slopes matches the description of his friends, he probably would have had time to kill Piney and still make it to the rendezvous point at the front of the pack. In fact, a delay makes sense. Everyone agreed he was the fastest, but they agreed he arrived at the chopper after Lucas, who was first."

"During your interviews, did anyone mention Piney's overall mood or behavior before heading down the mountain?" Landon asked. "Was he preoccupied? Nervous? Fearful?"

Houston hadn't brought up the subject of Piney's mood, but it was a good question for the next round of interviews. Landon also asked about Piney's private life, suggesting a complete background check might be helpful.

I focused my attention on Landon. "I was actually going to suggest you might want to do a search in addition to the one conducted by Houston and try to determine where the men crossed paths over the years as adults."

Landon looked at Houston. "Do you mind?"

"Not at all. I'm under no illusion that your hacker skills by far surpass mine, and the more information we have, the quicker we'll find the killer. If it turns out that there's any illegal hacking involved, I don't want to know."

Landon looked back at me. "Okay. I'll see what I can find."

"Let's discuss your results when you have them. I'd come to your place to talk, but I have kittens to care for. Do you want to come to my cabin for dinner?"

"Yeah, I can do that."

"Can you bring dinner?" I asked with a smile on my face.

Landon laughed. "Sure." He looked at Sarge. "Can you hook me up?"

Sarge nodded. "I have leftover soup in the refrigerator, and there are rolls you can heat up in the freezer."

"I'll bring something to go with the soup," Houston stated. "I appreciate the help, but I should be the one to steer the investigation as it unfolds."

"Fine by me," I said.

Landon sat back and narrowed his gaze. He didn't comment, but it seemed as if he had something on his mind. If I knew him, he was already using his superbrain to assemble the various pieces of this puzzle.

******

I decided to pick up a bit and then see to the needs of my menagerie before Landon and Houston arrived for our sleuthing session. Grabbing a heavy knit cap, my mukluks, and my rifle, I headed out with the seven dogs. The minute we left the yard and entered the forest, I could feel all the dogs going on high alert. Yukon and Denali, who usually ran ahead, chose to stay back with Lucky, Honey, and me, as did Shia, Kodi, and Juno. Walking with seven dogs in such close proximity was a bit crowded but comforting as well.

"What do you sense?" I asked Denali. There were times like this when I wished he could answer me. While Yukon was a highly trained search-and-rescue dog with mad skills, Denali was my guardian and protector.

Denali growled deep in his throat but continued to walk. I figured while he felt something, we weren't in immediate danger, so I tightened my grip on my rifle and followed his lead. It did occur to me that whoever had killed Piney might not want me snooping around, but with seven dogs, I didn't feel particularly threatened, especially by a group of city boys who'd gone on a ski trip, so I went forward, trying to put the thought in the back of my mind.

I was almost to the point where I planned to turn around when I heard a rustling in the bushes. The dogs didn't seem alarmed, so I assumed it was a rabbit or some other small animal. I paused to make sure nothing was going to jump out at me, then called to the dogs and slowly turned around to make my way back to the cabin. When we were halfway there, Denali let out a happy yip, then took off at a pace that could only be described as a homestretch run.

"I wonder what that was all about," I asked Yukon. He wagged his tail but didn't seem overly concerned. I glanced down at Honey, who looked as if she was smiling. "Do you know what that was all about?" Honey looked up at me. She put a paw on my thigh as if to ask permission to join her buddy. "Okay. Go on ahead."

Jake must have decided to attend the dinner meeting with Landon, Houston, and me. Denali didn't like many people. At least not enough to take off running, though Jake was one of the few he seemed to enjoy being around.

When I arrived at the cabin I found Honey along with another wrapped package on my porch. Denali was nowhere to be found so I let out a loud whistle to call him back from wherever he had gone off to. The fact that someone had dropped off the package and Denali had sensed a presence and had taken off to greet the gift giver, confirmed in my mind that the lights I'd received along with whatever was in this box could only be from Jake. If Chloe or Landon had left the gifts, Denali would have been alerted, but he wouldn't have taken off to say hi.

"Where'd you go?" I asked Denali when he came running back. "Is Jake hiding somewhere until I go inside?"

Denali wagged his tail.

"I don't know what's up with all the secrecy. If he knew I needed lights and wanted me to have them, why wouldn't he just give them to me?"

Denali barked once. I looked into the distance but didn't see anyone. I shrugged and went inside. The first thing I did was open the box, which contained a beautiful fir wreath that made me think of Harley, but Denali would more likely have barked and growled at Harley than greeted him happily, so I doubted he was my mystery Santa.

I found a nail and hung the wreath on my door, then headed out to the barn to see to the needs of Homer and the rabbits. Once they were fed and tucked in for the evening, I fed the dogs and cats, then went into the bedroom to see to the special feeding needs of the kittens. They sure were cute. Two were gray and white, one was black, one was orange, and the fifth was a brown-striped longhair that reminded me of Moose. Speaking of my cranky therapy cat, where was he? It occurred to me that he hadn't been in the kitchen with the other animals when I'd fed everyone.

"Moose," I called. "Here kitty, kitty." Moose wasn't the affectionate sort when he wasn't on duty and kept to himself a lot of the time, but he usually showed up when I called him. "Moose. Are you hiding? Come on out. It's time for dinner."

I looked high and low, but he didn't seem to be anywhere. Now I was getting worried. Could he have gotten out? He was independent and liked to live by his own rules and timetable, but he usually stayed close to home, especially when it was cold and the ground was covered with snow. Perhaps he'd followed me out to the barn without my seeing him. Could I have locked him in the barn? I grabbed my jacket and my rifle and went back out again. As I had in the house, I searched high and low; again, I found nothing.

Returning to the cabin, I opened the front door to find Moose sitting in the entry. "What the heck. Where were you?"

"Meow."

I picked him up and realized his paws were wet, with small balls of snow caked on his underbelly.

He'd been outside? Someone must have put him back in. The question was, who? I glanced around the room. Juno and Kodi were already settled in the barn, Honey and Lucky had most likely retired to the bedroom with the kittens, Yukon was sound asleep on the sofa, and Denali was stretched out by the fire. Okay, it was official; I was losing my mind. If anyone had opened the door to let Moose in other than possibly Jake, Denali would've had a fit, yet there he was lounging by the fire as if nothing had happened.

Grabbing a towel from the laundry room, I dried Moose off, gave him a cuddle, and sat him down next to Yukon on the sofa. Houston and Landon would be here any moment and I still needed to wash up, so the case of where Moose had been was one mystery that might never be solved.

******

I was starving by the time Landon showed up with the soup and rolls he'd gotten from Sarge and Houston arrived with a huge salad it looked like he'd made himself and a cake he must have bought at the Christmas festival. We decided to eat while we talked.

"I started with a rudimentary search of all six men," Landon informed us as we served up plates of food and settled around the dining table. "So far, I've found three instances when two or more of them worked together on a project."

"What were the projects?" I asked as I dipped a roll into my soup.

"The oldest was five years ago. The men were fresh out of college and, I assume, raring to make their mark. They teamed up to tackle a very impressive condo project. Reggie, you remember, went into investment banking and was able to line up some investors. Colin, the commercial real estate agent, found the perfect piece of land. Anton, the accountant, worked out the budget and kept track of the expenses as well as the projected income. Drake's company developed the project, which was built by Lucas's company, and when the units were ready, Colin sold them."

"What about Piney?" I asked.

"I'm not sure. I didn't find any mention of his name. Perhaps he wasn't involved. It seems likely he would have still been in law school then. Colin went into real estate right out of high school, skipping college, so he would have already been working in his field for a few years when the opportunity came up. Lucas also skipped college and went to work on a contractor's license, which he was able to obtain fairly quickly because he worked construction all through high school and had a lot of work experience hours. Reggie was working on his MBA while the project was being developed, but he already had contacts, which he utilized to come up with the money they needed. Anton and Drake had both recently graduated from college and were working for large firms."

"And how did the project do?" Houston asked.

"As far as I can tell from a cursory look, really well. It appeared they all made a bundle. I suspect this success led to their working together on another project two years later. This time they built a strip mall. Again, I found mention of Colin, Reggie, Drake, Lucas, and Anton, but not Piney. I suspect

Piney would have had his law degree by then, but he would have been just starting out, so perhaps the timing wasn't the best for his inclusion. He was involved in the most recent project Drake and Reggie teamed up on, though."

I realized that must be the one Anabelle had talked about. "What is it?"

"Drake is developing low-income housing. I didn't find reference to Colin, Lucas, or Anton, but Reggie lined up the financing and Piney was overseeing the permit process, which sounds like it was turning out to be quite a minefield."

I remembered my own attempts to get funding for the shelter before Harley donated the building. Talk about a convoluted process.

"Because Piney is the one who's dead, if their business dealings turned out to be the motive, it's this most recent project we should focus on," Houston suggested.

"Perhaps," Landon said. "I found something else too however. Something I haven't had a chance to really look in to."

"What is that?" Houston asked.

"It appears as if the law firm Piney worked for is involved in the defense of a real estate developer in a class action lawsuit. I don't know if that relates to Drake's company or not, but I'll follow up to see what else I can find out."

After dinner, Houston helped me clean up while Landon continued to work. He put in an hour of digging and then told us the lawsuit Piney's firm was involved in defending was against Drake's company. The plaintiffs claimed they'd purchased condominiums in good faith, but they were built using shoddy material. The structures were literally falling down. Landon continued to search and was eventually able to verify that the class action suit had been initiated by the homeowners who'd purchased units in the first development the guys built together.

"So if Piney's firm was defending Drake and the others, how does he end up dead?" I asked. "If it was the other way around and he was representing the plaintiffs, I could see a motive."

"I don't know," Landon said, "but I'm going to keep looking."

"Perhaps I should have another chat with Drake," Houston said.

"I doubt he'll tell you anything," Landon said. "He's being sued. I bet he's been counseled to keep his mouth shut."

"A man died," I pointed out.

"And there's every indication that one of the men involved in the lawsuit killed him," Landon insisted.

"Landon's right," Houston said. "Drake isn't going to talk. But maybe one of the others will. Anton was the accountant; if they were cutting corners, chances are he was in on it. Colin sold the units. It was his job to verify the construction reports. Of course, that doesn't mean he did so. Lucas actually built the units, so he's in this up to his armpits. Reggie's the one who persuaded his contacts to invest in the project. I imagine he's not too happy about the way things turned out. His investors must want to string him alive."

I looked at Landon. "Do you know when the lawsuit was brought against Drake's company?"

Landon typed in some commands. "Four months ago."

"Was that before or after the low-income housing project got underway?"

"After. They've been working on this latest project for a while now. I'd bet this lawsuit isn't going to help the permit process."

I picked up my small mama cat, Lucy, who'd wandered over. "I don't know what's going on, but I sense a motive in all this mess."

"I agree." Houston stood up. "I know Drake probably won't talk to me again, but I'm going to take a stab at Reggie. He's most likely in the same pot of boiling water as everyone else, but he may be the only one who didn't know what was going on all along."

Landon worked a while longer after Houston left but then announced he'd continue his search from home. As he packed up, he noticed the lights on my counter. "I see you decided to get lights after all."

"Actually, they were a gift."

"Really? From whom?"

"I don't know. It occurred to me that you were my secret Santa because we talked about my decorations going up with the barn."

"I wish I had been your secret Santa, but I'm not. Maybe Jake?"

"That's my best guess. He's been going decoration crazy and might have realized mine were destroyed in the fire, but I don't get keeping it a secret. Jake is usually the sort to notice when I need something, and then he just gives it to me. Like when I needed new tires, he took my Jeep, and the next thing I knew, I had new tires. If my roof leaks, he comes by to fix it. If Jake was behind the lights, I'd more likely come home from work and find them hung on the front of the cabin."

"Maybe it isn't Jake. Wyatt?"

I raised a brow.

"You're right. Being a secret Santa would never occur to him. Chloe?"

I shrugged. "Maybe."

Landon picked up one of the strings I'd stacked four high. "Do you want help hanging them?"

"It's dark."

"True. But we have two vehicles with headlights. We can do the front of the cabin. Maybe hang lights along the roofline and around the window and door."

I smiled. "If you really want to help, I'd love to get them up. You grab the ladder and I'll get some cocoa."

Chapter 7

Monday, December 17

I woke to huge snowflakes drifting softly on the still air. During the winter, the bar was closed on Sundays and Mondays, which meant I had the entire day off to do as I pleased. Houston and I had set up a routine of spending at least a couple of hours working with Kojak on search-and-rescue training on Monday afternoons. I probably should have confirmed his intention to meet for a session today when he was here last night.

In the meantime, I had my own dogs to walk, and the foster Harley was temporarily housing to work with on basic commands and appropriate behavior. I glanced out the window at the gently falling snow and fought the urge to pull the covers over my head and go back to sleep. I'd enjoy a lazy morning in bed, but the dogs would gang up on me in revolt if I didn't take them out soon. In addition to walking the dogs, I had animals to feed and cat boxes and barn stalls to clean. Even a day off was a busy day for me.

"I see you moved your temporary family to the bed," I said to Honey, who was curled up on top of the covers next to me with the five kittens. They sure looked content snuggled in between her legs. I hated to disturb them, but duty called.

Honey lifted her head and thumped her tail when she noticed me watching. She really was the sweetest dog. There were those who felt she was lucky to have found me, but I knew without a doubt it was the other way around.

"It's fine," I said to Honey as she bent over and nosed her honorary babies. "I don't mind sharing, but it's time to get up and feed everyone." I slipped out of bed, pulled a heavy sweatshirt over the long johns I'd worn to bed, then slipped my feet into knee-high slippers. The other dogs in the room began to stir, so I began putting kittens on the floor, then led everyone out to the main living area, where I found Denali curled up next to the front door. Always the protector.

I tossed several logs on the fire, which had burned down to embers overnight, fed the cats and kittens, and then headed back into the bedroom to get dressed. After pulling on a pair of jeans, a flannel shirt, heavy boots, and a warm jacket, I pulled a stocking cap onto my head and grabbed my rifle. I called the dogs to the back door. Before setting off into the dark morning, I stopped off at the barn to pick up Kodi and Juno.

As I trudged through the forest with my flashlight to show me the way, I noticed the new layer of snow covering most of the tracks the dogs and I had left in previous walks along the familiar path. The fresh snow and lack of old tracks was most likely the only reason I happened to notice the fresh ones, which I was certain must have been left after our last walk the night before.

I glanced at Denali, who was wagging his tail and trotting along as if he didn't have a care in the world. Odd. Everything I knew about the dog told me that he should be barking, growling, and having a fit because someone had dared venture so close to the cabin. The fact that he wasn't upset in the least both intrigued and frightened me. Who could have made the tracks in the middle of the night without alerting the dogs?

I paused and bent down for a closer look. I took the glove off my right hand and used one finger to lightly brush the new snow from the evenly spaced footsteps. The prints were obviously made by male-sized snow boots, at least an eleven, and from the amount of snow covering them, I had to assume they'd been made between one and two hours ago. The dogs in the house had been fast asleep an hour ago, so it was possible the visitor could have snuck past the cabin without alerting Honey, Lucky, Shia, and even Yukon. But Denali? Denali heard and sensed everyone and everything. Even the predators the others missed completely. It was highly unlikely someone had come this close to the cabin without him sensing them.

I tried to figure out the path from the prints. It looked as if whoever had made them had come from the forest and circled around to the front of the cabin on the far side of the property, away from the barn. That made sense, especially if the visitor knew there were dogs sleeping in the barn. I debated whether to follow the tracks into the forest to find the origin of the footprints or go back to the cabin to confirm my suspicion that the person who'd made them was my secret Santa. Given that it was still pitch black out and snow was continuing to fall, I decided to go back home, but if the prints were still visible after the sun rose, I fully intended to take a closer look.

As I suspected there would be, there was a package wrapped in green paper on my porch. I took it inside and opened it right away to find several strings of brightly colored tree lights. I smiled as I let the romance of the experience soften the rough edges around my heart. Part of me was touched and extremely grateful to my secret Santa, while another was frustrated with the anonymity of the gift giver. I hadn't planned to cut a tree this year, but now that I had lights to make it pretty...

I clicked on some Christmas music and glided around the room after I fed the dogs, trying to puzzle out who could be leaving the gifts. The fact that Denali hadn't tried to rip them to shreds really did just leave Jake, though there was no way he'd be tromping through the woods to deliver a package before the sun even began its ascent. Jake was giving and kindhearted, and I was certain if he'd realized I wanted and needed decorations, he'd buy them for me in a heartbeat. But he wouldn't deliver the packages this way. My mind told me it had to be Jake, but my instinct said it wasn't.

But if not Jake, who? I poured myself a cup of coffee, then sat down in front of the fire to drink it. Chloe was my best friend and, like Jake, would happily buy lights for me if I expressed a desire for them. Of course, things were just as tight financially for her during the winter as they were for me, and there was even less of a chance she'd tromp around in the forest in the middle of the night to deliver them. Landon was a sweet guy who always seemed to have money, but he'd said he hadn't left the packages, and I believed him. Harley, like the others, was kind and giving and would totally be the sort to think of something so sweet and thoughtful, but he had a pup-size chewing machine to worry about, so I couldn't imagine him taking an early morning stroll through the snowy forest.

I sipped my coffee and tried to go more deeply into my friends list. I knew a lot of people in Rescue, but I couldn't think of a single one who would do what my secret Santa had been doing. I supposed there was Houston, but he was even less in to Christmas than I was. That left... no one. I couldn't think of anyone who would have delivered Christmas decorations to me in what was almost the middle of the night.

Still, the gifts were fun. I smiled as I lifted the lights out of the box. I thought of Nick Clauston's encounter with the "real Santa," and for a brief moment I let myself consider the possibility that my early gifts might have been delivered by the jolly old man in red himself.

******

I cleaned the barn and the cat boxes and drove over to Harley's. I'd called Houston to confirm that he'd meet me around noon for Kojak's training session, which left me a good three hours to call in a favor, put my training session into play, and to work with Brando on some basic commands. I wanted to check in at the shelter before heading over to Houston's office, but that wouldn't take long. I hoped Harley wasn't having too difficult a time with the energetic pup. He'd been such a good sport, agreeing to take him, and he'd already done so much for the strays in town. I hated to take advantage of his good nature.

I found Harley outside with Brando, playing tug-of-war with a thick rope. Both man and dog seemed to be having a wonderful time. I smiled as I parked my old Jeep and climbed out.

"It looks like you're having fun," I said as the pup ran to me. I could see he intended to jump up on my leg, so I took a step forward, which caused him to stop running and sit in front of me. "Good boy, Brando. Nice greeting, buddy." I ruffled the dog's ears, then gave him a treat I had stored in my pocket.

"How do you get him to sit every time?" Harley asked. "He jumps all over me."

"I step into his path, which interrupts his momentum and makes him sit. Learning not to jump up is an important thing to teach a pup. At least in the beginning. After he gets older and can begin to discriminate between welcome and unwelcome jumping up, you can teach him the jump up command."

"Why would I want him to ever jump up?"

"Some people enjoy being greeted that way, and it's fine for a dog to do it if invited. But at this point it's best to teach him to sit when he approaches a person. He's going to be a big dog and you don't want him jumping up on every person he encounters."

Harley lifted a brow. "You talk about this eating and chewing machine as if I'm going to have him with me when he is a full-grown dog."

I smiled. "Not at all. I was referring to the universal you." The pup got up and ran back over to the rope. "Should we get started?"

"I've been playing with him for a good thirty minutes, so hopefully, he'll be tired out a bit and willing to pay attention. Is that Yukon in your Jeep?"

"It is. I brought him along to help with the training. I'll fetch him and you go get Brando's leash."

Brando adored Yukon and was more than happy to ape his every move. When I asked Yukon to heel, Brando fell into line alongside us. When I gave Yukon the command to come, Brando followed happily along. He likewise sat and stayed when Yukon did so. I knew that at some point we'd need to remove Yukon from the sessions, but for an introductory lesson, Yukon's example was invaluable. After we'd run through commands for about thirty minutes, we went inside to give the dogs a rest and the people a chance to warm up. Harley poured me a cup of coffee as Brando and Yukon settled by the fire.

"Brando's picking up on the training commands pretty quickly," he said.

"He's doing a wonderful job," I agreed.

Harley grinned. "I knew he was smart. Maybe I can train him to be a stunt dog."

"It appears Brando has a strong play instinct, and he wants to please you. If you decide to keep him, and really do want to train him as a stunt dog, I think he'll be an excellent one. It seems to me, based on what we've done so far, he'd probably make a good service dog as well."

Harley glanced at Brando, who was curled up with Yukon. I couldn't help but notice a softening in his eyes.

"How'd he do last night?" I asked.

"He woke up once, around two. I took him out and he peed, then came right in and went back to sleep. He didn't wake up again until I went to him at around eight. I'd prefer it if he slept all the way through the night, of course, but I felt like he did pretty well."

"I think he did very well too. He's still young and may not have the bladder control you'd like quite yet, but if you limit his water after seven and take him out right before you go to bed, I think he'll make it through the night. Has he chewed anything else?"

"Just a sofa pillow. I still don't know how he got hold of it. I was sitting in the den watching a movie and he was sleeping at my feet. I might have dozed off for just a minute because I never even saw him get up and pull the pillow down."

"Sounds like he woke up and got bored. A bored puppy is a destructive puppy, but we can work on helping him to understand what it's okay to chew on and what he can't once we finish our coffee. You bought him a lot of toys and rawhide bones you can distribute around the house. When he learns to discriminate, he should do better about inappropriate chewing."

After we finished our coffee, I showed Harley how to correct and replace when Brando went for an object that wasn't his to chew. We used a pot holder, a sock, and a pillow as temptations. When he went for them, he was corrected and told that they didn't belong to him. Then we replaced those items with one of his toys to chew on and carry around. Harley had been right from the beginning; Brando *was* smart. Thirty minutes and a handful of treats later, he was able to respond to a cue to get his toy. When I returned the next day, we'd work on the command to "leave it."

At Harley's I noticed he'd placed several real trees around the house that he'd decorated like Christmas trees, small firs he planned to plant in the yard when the ground thawed in the spring. On impulse, I asked him if I could buy one of them from him so I could give it to Houston for his office. I suspected he hadn't done a thing to decorate, and for some reason, I felt bad he hadn't found a way to embrace the holiday spirit, even though I'd gone years after my parents' death avoiding the trappings, much the way he was doing now. Harley, being the generous guy he was, gave me two of his little trees, one for Houston and one for my dining table at home.

After thanking him and promising to come back the next day, I headed to the shelter. The volunteers on duty assured me everything was fine, so I took my dog and my little tree home, and then headed to Houston's office for our usual Monday training session.

Chapter 8

"I've come bearing gifts," I said to Houston, placing the small decorated tree on his desk. "I know you aren't really in to the holiday thing, but we wouldn't want the residents of Rescue to think their chief of police was a Grinch, would we?"

Houston glanced at the tree and then back at me. "You bought me a Christmas tree?"

"Actually, this is one of Harley's trees; he has a bunch and he said it was fine." I adjusted the tree just a bit so the ornaments were displayed in the most pleasing manner. "There. A little Christmas cheer for your office, and the best thing is that it's a real tree you can plant outdoors in the spring."

"So I'm going to need to water the tree until then? Seems like more of an obligation than a gift."

I shrugged. "It's a little tree. I doubt keeping it alive will be too taxing. Are you ready to head out?"

"Almost. I just need to finish my notes on my follow-up interviews with the ski group."

I sat down at the desk across from Houston. "Did you learn anything new from the interviews?"

"From the interviews, no. The men seemed to have clammed up more than they did that first day. I did find out from the guys at the lab that the blow to Piney's throat, which sliced through his windpipe and has been confirmed to be the cause of death, looks to have been delivered by someone who thrust the ski pole into his neck with his left hand. When I was at the inn this morning, I noticed the only left-handed member of the group is Reggie."

"So Reggie must have killed Piney."

"That's what I'm thinking," Houston confirmed. "He was the one who organized the trip, and he also admitted to being the one who paid for Piney to come because he was unable to afford the trip on his own. I suppose it could be argued that he set things up to create a situation in which he could make it look as if Piney had gotten lost and fallen to his death."

I frowned. "That makes sense to a point, but why? If Reggie wanted to kill Piney for some reason, why go to all the expense of bringing him here? Why not just kill him at home, wherever home is."

"The men all live in the Seattle area. And in answer to your question, I don't know why. And I'm going to need more than a hunch based on hand preference to arrest Reggie. So far, I don't have more."

I sat back in my chair and considered the situation. "We can figure this out. Let's go back through what we know to see if we can come up with a motive. We know Reggie and Piney have worked together on several projects."

"Actually, we don't know that," Houston corrected me. "Landon found evidence that Reggie worked with Drake, Anton, Lucas, and Colin on past projects, and he's currently working with Drake on the low-income housing. It appears Piney may be involved in that, but we don't know for certain, and there's no evidence he was involved in prior projects."

I frowned. "Yeah, you're right. We decided Piney was most likely still in law school when the other projects were developed. It appears the law firm Piney works for is defending the other five in the class-action lawsuit that's been brought. Maybe Piney knew something pertaining to it. Maybe he had damaging evidence that would have cost the others dearly, and they didn't trust him to keep it to himself because he wasn't personally involved, so they killed him. Or Reggie killed him on behalf of the group."

Houston leaned forward on his forearms. "Then why the ski trip? Why Alaska? Again, I have to wonder why Reggie or the group or whoever wanted Piney dead, would bring him all the way here to kill him. Killing him in such an isolated situation makes the five others look guilty."

I bit my lower lip. "Yeah, you have a point. If one of his friends wanted him dead, it would have been a lot smarter to shoot him while he walked the streets of Seattle. Why bring him here to do it when that would call attention to the members of the group?" I glanced out the window. It looked like the snow had stopped, at least for the moment. That was good, I supposed. "Still," I said, "despite the fact that it makes no sense one of six friends who were on a ski trip would be killed by another in that specific time and place, it stands to reason that's what happened. I honestly doubt anyone else was there on the mountain."

"What if it wasn't premeditated?" Houston asked. "What if something happened while they were on the mountain that caused one of them to stab Piney in the throat with the sharp end of a ski pole?"

"Did the lab find blood on any of the poles?"

Houston shook his head. "No. But that doesn't mean one of the men didn't kill Piney. There was time for the pole to have been bleached clean or even replaced. I probably should have collected everyone's ski gear right off the bat, but I didn't know Piney had been murdered when we brought the others down the mountain."

I steepled my fingers, then rhythmically tapped my tips together. "Okay, so how do we figure this out? The odds are very much in favor of Reggie, Drake, Anton, Lucas, or Colin being the killer. We suspect Reggie based on his left-handedness. In my opinion, all of them seemed to be either lying or at least protecting the truth when you spoke to him the day of the murder. I can't say one stood out over the others as being the probable killer other than that. The fact that they did business together and money was involved in their relationship, lends itself to motive, especially given the large dollar amounts involved in these projects." I took a moment to gather my thoughts. "Reggie is the money man. It stands to reason he could conceivably have the most to lose if things went south. He's the one who brought in the investors. I'm sure those investors aren't happy that something has happened that might cost them their investment."

"A lawsuit that seems to point toward negligence would do that."

"Exactly. Still, Piney's firm is representing the defendants. Even if he had proof of misconduct on the part of the contractor, developer, or others, it seems as if attorney/client confidentiality would prevent him from sharing what he knows. There has to be something else going on. Something that would lend itself to an act of rage. That's the only thing that really makes sense given the timing of the murder."

Houston sat back in his chair. "I suspect one or more of the group have an idea who the killer might be. I need to find a way to get them to open up about whatever they're obviously trying to hide."

I stood up and paced around the room. "What if you lie? What if you speak to each man separately, and during the course of that interview, we tell each one that Piney has been murdered and he's been fingered by his friends as the killer? That might cause one of them to spill it if they know something."

"Sure, if they've never watched a cop show on TV. Seems contrived, and these men are both smart and sophisticated."

I sat back down. "I guess you're right. If they're all in on this, they probably have their stories down pat. What about physical evidence on Piney's body? Might he have struggled with the person who killed him? Maybe there's DNA evidence under his fingernails."

"The medical examiner is looking for that, and the crime lab is going over the clothes he was wearing. If there's evidence, they'll find it, but so far, they're coming up dry."

It seemed finding out who killed Piney was both easy and complicated at the same time. On one hand, we only had five suspects, which would seem to make finding the killer easier than some cases Houston and I had worked on together. On the other hand, there didn't seem to be a way to conclusively identify which man was the killer, and the fact that all the men seemed to be lying was making it even harder to herd out the guilty party. Reggie as the killer made a lot of sense, but I was far from feeling confident about that conclusion. The whole thing was giving me a headache. I glanced at Kojak, who was still curled up next to Houston's feet. "Do you still want to go out?"

"Yeah, let's go. Maybe the fresh air will clear my mind."

I'd decided it was time to try a long-distance retrieval with Kojak, so I'd had Wyatt walk a route I provided that would take us deep into the woods. At the end of the trail, he'd left clothes he'd worn recently. I also had several pieces of clothing with his scent on them that I'd have Houston use to provide Kojak with the scent he was to follow. The dog was doing so well, I felt he was ready for this test despite his young age.

I handed Houston the plastic bag with Wyatt's undershirt in it. "Today we're looking for Wyatt. Or at least Wyatt's clothes. You'll provide Kojak with the scent and then tell him to find Wyatt, just like we did on shorter retrievals. Wyatt walked the route I gave him before I showed up at your place, so the scent should be fresh."

"What if he heads in the wrong direction?" Houston asked.

"We'll give him a minute to self-correct. If he doesn't, you'll give him the scent and the command to find Wyatt again. If he still can't find the correct direction, you'll provide a hint to get him going. Ready?"

Houston nodded. He looked as nervous as Kojak looked excited. I understood that. I remembered being nervous about Yukon's first big test when Jake was helping me train him.

Houston took the undershirt out of the bag. "Kojak, this is Wyatt. We need to find Wyatt." He let the dog take a good long sniff. "Find Wyatt."

Kojak sniffed the air and the ground and then took off to the north. Houston glanced at me. I nodded. It was important for Houston not to know the location of the clothes so he didn't unintentionally provide subtle clues to Kojak that wouldn't be available to him in a real rescue.

Kojak traveled for about a quarter mile in the correct direction before he paused and looked around. I almost laughed at his expression, which seemed to say he suddenly had no idea what he was supposed to be doing. "Give him the scent and the command to find Wyatt again," I told Houston.

He took the shirt out of the bag. "Kojak, this is Wyatt. Find Wyatt."

Kojak took another good sniff, then sniffed the area for a couple of minutes. Eventually, he continued on his way. Houston looked at me once again, and once again, I nodded. The dog was nailing this test. It wouldn't be long before our two-dog search-and-rescue team would have three dogs. It was important to have as many dog and human rescue teams as we could manage to train. During the worst storms of the season, it wasn't unheard of to have two or even three rescues going on at the same time. The most dangerous storms seemed to come early in the season, storms that came at the end of a day that had started off sunny. Storms that left hikers and skiers unprepared for the change in weather most never saw coming.

When Kojak was less than a quarter mile away from the spot where I'd had Wyatt leave the clothes, he stopped walking. He sniffed the air, then began to growl. Houston looked at me and asked what he should do. I was about to tell him to give Kojak the scent again when I had a flash.

"Wait," I said as I paused and closed my eyes.

"What is it?" Houston asked.

"Put Kojak on the leash," I said in a voice so quiet I was surprised Houston heard it.

"Do you sense something?" Houston asked, as he clipped the leash onto Kojak, then scratched his ears to calm him. Kojak let out two loud barks before Houston was able to command him to be quiet. Kojak was still growling from deep in his chest, but he was obeying Houston's command and didn't bark again. "Is someone in trouble?" Houston asked.

I nodded. I didn't want to speak or open my eyes. I knew from experience that doing either could cause me to lose the connection I'd established if it wasn't a strong one.

"Someone's in trouble," I said after a minute.

"Someone close by?"

I nodded. After a moment, I opened my eyes. I put my hand to my throat. I could feel the burning. I gasped as I found myself unable to breathe.

"Harm, are you okay?" Houston said in a panic. "What can I do?"

I held up my hand. As quickly as it began, it was over. I took several breaths of the cold, crisp air and looked around. The forest was dense and I couldn't see much more than snow and trees. I closed my eyes again and tried to bring back the image. The connection had been brief and I hadn't seen much, but I had the sense of a rock cropping nearby. I looked as far into the distance as I could and pointed. "There. We need to look there."

"Look?" Houston asked. "Look for what?"

"The man or woman who just killed the person I was momentarily connected with."

Houston pulled out his gun and handed me Kojak's leash. "Killed?" he said. "Does that mean it's too late to save the victim?"

"I think so. I felt someone struggling to breathe and then they were gone."

"Maybe you should wait here," Houston suggested.

"No. We'll go together."

I could see Houston wanted to argue, but he must have realized I'd probably be safer with him and his gun because he nodded and motioned for me to follow him. I walked quietly toward the rock cropping I'd sensed. It didn't take long to find the man who'd had his throat slit, lying in a pool of blood soaking into the snow.

"It's Reggie Slater," Houston said.

I nodded.

"And the killer?" Houston asked.

"Gone." I looked toward the nearby clearing and pointed to tracks in the snow. Tracks made by a sleigh that had been pulled by two reindeer.

Chapter 9

By the time I made it home it was dark. It had been hours since the dogs had been out, so I grabbed my rifle and the five dogs who preferred the comfort of the house, then went to the barn to pick up Kodi and Juno. I was cold and wet and exhausted, so my plan was to take the dogs for a short walk, then go back to the cabin for a hot shower and something even hotter to eat. Probably soup; I was pretty sure that was all I had on hand. I wasn't much of a cook, and more often than not I ate at Neverland anyway, so most of the time my lack of culinary skill didn't matter.

The dogs and I were halfway back to the cabin when Denali let out a happy yip and took off running. What the—? Maybe my secret Santa had been slipping steaks to my guard dog. Denali took his job as my guardian seriously and was never all that happy to see anyone. Anyone except…

"No," I said out loud to myself. The only person who would send Denali into fits of joy was a long-haired mystery man from a tropical climate who'd visited for just a short time but had made a huge impact on my life and the life of my most ferocious dog. Calling the other dogs to my side, I picked up the pace. When I arrived at the cabin, I found yet another package wrapped in green paper. I didn't see Denali anywhere, so I let out a loud whistle and waited. After a few minutes, he came trotting over and sat down next to me.

"Shredder is my secret Santa, isn't he?"

Denali looked at me with an innocent expression, but the happy gleam in his eyes told me I was right.

"Shredder, are you out there?" I called into the darkness.

I waited, but he didn't answer, so I assumed he'd moved on. I couldn't imagine what he was doing here. Picking up the package, I went inside.

I'd first met Shredder the previous December, when a photo had brought him to Rescue in search of an international killer. I still wasn't certain who he worked for, but from the little bits I'd picked up along the way, I was guessing some black ops division of the FBI, CIA, or similar agency. He seemed to have connections all over the world but didn't actually live anywhere or answer to anyone, at least not to anyone he could or would identify. The first time I'd met him, I'd tried to get more information out of him, but he was skilled at sharing only what he wanted to share. Initially, I hadn't trusted him—he'd simply let himself into my cabin while I'd been out with the dogs—but then he helped me deliver Honey's puppies, and I'd decided anyone who would pull pups from a dog he'd just met couldn't be all bad. When I arrived at the cabin, I found Honey sitting on Shredder's lap, and she'd gone into labor soon after that. My mystery man had helped me ensure the health of both mom and pups. Delivering puppies with a man I'd just met wasn't the most surprising thing that happened that day. That was when Denali, who doesn't trust anyone, acted like a puppy being reunited with his long-lost owner. Not only hadn't he torn Shredder a new one for sneaking into the cabin, he had been thrilled to see him.

Deciding to change into dry clothes before I did anything else, I headed into my bedroom, mulling over the situation. The only person who could be delivering the packages without being mauled by Denali, other than Jake, was Shredder, but it made no sense that he would be here in Rescue. Unless he was on another mission. But if that was the case, I'd think he'd make himself known rather than sneaking around the way my secret Santa was.

Once I'd changed, I went into the kitchen to hunt up that soup. I'd just opened the cabinet when my phone rang.

"Hey, Houston. Any news on Reggie's murder?"

"Reggie's murder, no, but I may have a degree of proof, or at least an arguable motive, for who killed Piney and why. I was just about to grab some dinner. Do you want to join me? We can talk about the new information while we eat."

I looked at the animals, who must already feel deserted because I'd been gone all day. "If you wouldn't mind picking something up and bringing it here, I'd be up for that. I still need to feed the animals and clean the cat boxes and the barn."

"I can do that. What would you like?"

"Normally, I just get takeout from Neverland, but it's closed. There is a new pizza place in town if you like pizza."

"I know the place. What toppings do you like?"

"I'm not picky; you choose."

"Okay. I'll see you in about thirty minutes."

I fed the cats and dogs who lived in the house, then walked Kodi and Juno back to the barn and fed them, as well as Homer and the rabbits. By the time I'd cleaned Homer's stall and spent a few minutes with each animal, close to thirty minutes had passed. In the cabin, I cleaned the cat boxes and washed up. I was just drying my hands when Houston pulled up with Kojak.

"Meat Lover's Dream," I said after opening the pizza box. "It looks delicious. I'm starving."

I took two plates out of the cupboard and set them on the table. "I have beer, milk, or cola. Or I can make a pot of coffee."

"I usually have beer with pizza, but tonight I'll just have a cola. I still have quite a bit of work to do."

I pulled two cans of cola out of the refrigerator and took them to the table. "So what evidence did you come up with?" I asked as I slid a large slice onto my plate.

Houston took a bite of his pizza, chewed, and swallowed before he answered. "Reggie's phone was on him. It was unlocked, and it appeared as if he, or someone else, had been looking at the document that was pulled up when he was attacked."

"What document?"

"A text with several attachments." Houston took a sip of his soda. "The text was sent to Reggie on the day the group went up to the mountain to ski. It read, 'Here's the proof you requested.' Attached were several emails sent between Piney and someone named Armand Cole. I've since discovered he's one of the attorneys representing the group behind the lawsuit."

I frowned. "Wait: Piney works for the law firm defending Drake and the others, yet he was communicating with one of the attorneys on the opposing team?"

"That's the way it looks."

"Dare I ask about the content of the emails?"

"Basically," Houston said, "they contain copies of photos, invoices, and internal communications between Drake, Reggie, and Lucas that prove all three were aware subpar materials were being used for the project to cut costs. The documents are incriminating enough that the three of them could be looking at jailtime."

"Why?" I questioned. "Why would Piney turn these documents over to opposing counsel?"

"For money," Houston answered before taking another bite of his pizza. "From what I've already dug up, Piney was an unspectacular business attorney who didn't have a lot of prospects for the future. His student loans were strangling him, and he was struggling to make a mark for himself in his chosen field and to keep up with his more successful friends. When Landon was here the other night, he mentioned that Reggie paid for him to come on this trip as well as others the group took."

"It sounds like Reggie was a good friend. Why would he want to stab him in the back?"

"I don't know. But Reggie received the text and the proof that Piney had agreed to sell very damaging information to the opposing attorney the day Piney died."

"So Reggie *did* kill him. I guess he must have felt betrayed when he found out what Piney was up to. I guess I don't blame him for wanting to protect his company and his freedom."

Houston set his slice down on his plate and wiped his hands with a napkin. "We both thought he did it; this just gives him a motive. Reggie must have pulled Piney aside and confronted him after the others began to spread out. I assume they argued, and Reggie's temper may have gotten the better of him. He stabbed Piney with his ski pole and sent him over the edge of the cliff. Of course, that's going to be hard to prove now that he's dead too."

"If Reggie killed Piney, who killed Reggie?" I wondered.

"That I don't know. Yet. But I intend to find out."

I had no idea where to even begin to look for Reggie's killer. It could have been one of the other four men, but I couldn't think of a reason any of them would. And then there were the sleigh tracks. How did a sleigh fit into things?

"It looks like you got another present," Houston said, nodding to the package on the counter when there was a lull in the conversation.

"It was on the porch when I got back from walking the dogs." I got up and crossed the room. I grabbed my scissors, then brought the package back to the table. "Christmas ornaments. I already received lights for a tree." I looked at Houston. "I don't suppose you'd be interested in going with me to find one? I hate to waste the lights and ornaments by not displaying them."

Houston lifted a shoulder. "I'll help you. Just let me know when you want to go." He sat back and looked at the colorful bulbs. "You still have no idea who's leaving these gifts for you?"

"No idea at all," I said because it was easier than trying to explain Shredder.

After Houston left, I took the dogs out for one last bathroom break before getting ready for bed. Denali once again took off when we were only halfway home, and I knew my secret Santa was back. Twice in one evening wasn't his usual pattern, so I thought something other than bringing gifts was behind this visit.

"I thought I would find you here," I said to the brown-eyed man who sat on my sofa with Denali in his lap.

"You did?"

I glanced at Denali. "There isn't another person alive, with the exception of Jake, who can walk into the cabin unannounced without getting a piece taken out of their hide. What are you doing here?"

He grinned. "I'm happy to see you too."

I couldn't help but laugh. I walked across the room and slipped onto Shredder's lap, shoving Denali slightly aside to do so. I put my arms around my mystery man's neck and gave him a hug. "You look good. The same." I put my hand on his cheek and looked into his eyes. "Less tan then when I saw you a year ago."

"Riptide and I no longer live in the tropics. We're currently in a place not much warmer than this. The tan has faded." Shredder nodded toward Honey, who'd wandered over and curled up on the rug in front of the fireplace with her five kittens. "Didn't I help deliver puppies when I was here last?"

I chuckled. "You did. And they grew up to be healthy and happy dogs, thanks to your help. They all found wonderful forever homes, but I kept Honey with me. I found these kittens in a box on my doorstep a few nights ago. I don't suppose you were the one who left them?"

Shredder shook his head. "Sorry, love. If I'd found kittens, I would have ensured they'd be okay and wouldn't have left them in a box on a doorstep. It looks like Honey is doing a good job being a surrogate mother."

"She is. And these aren't the first strays she's nurtured. She's a natural mother. She even fostered a baby bear cub for a little while this fall." I looked around for the Border collie Shredder took everywhere. "Where's Riptide?"

"With a friend. The situation I'm here to investigate required me to stay at the inn, which doesn't allow pets."

I slipped off Shredder's lap and sat down next to him on the sofa. "The inn? You must be the blond skier Mary referred to."

Shredder nodded.

"Piney and Reggie," I realized. "You must be here because of whatever's going on with Piney and Reggie." I frowned. "Why have you been lurking around? Why not just tell me you were here? And what's up with all the Christmas decorations?"

"I've been 'lurking around' because I wasn't supposed to tell anyone I was around, but I wanted to keep an eye on you. The gifts were an impulse, which is odd because I never give in to impulse. I noticed you didn't have lights on the cabin and I knew about the fire, so I put two and two together and realized your decorations must have been destroyed. I was here anyway, so I decided to have some fun with it."

"Fun?"

Shredder shrugged. "It was fun for me. Wasn't it fun for you?"

I tilted my head. "I guess it was fun, but I'm having a hard time wrapping my head around all this. How did you know about the fire?"

"I just said I've been keeping an eye on you."

I raised a brow. "Why? Have you been spying on me?"

Shredder laughed. "No, not spying. Until a few days ago, I hadn't been back to Alaska since I left last year. And no, I didn't leave listening devices around your house. But I have been keeping my eyes and ears open. You're an exceptional human with a knack for getting yourself into the middle of whatever's going on around you, so I make it a point of knowing how you're doing. Which, by the way, is why I almost showed up here in October, when you had all that trouble with the man who killed your friend. I'm sorry about that."

I frowned again. "It was a really bad situation. A lot of good people died. Why didn't you come?"

"I wanted to. I tried to. But I was held up with the Saudis in a not entirely pleasant situation. By the time I extricated myself from that little nightmare, you'd already saved the day on your own and there was no reason for me to ride up on my white horse."

I couldn't help but smile at the image of Shredder riding up on a horse. "You still could have come," I pointed out. "You could have shown up and given me a hug and said, 'Hey, Harm, I was worried about you. I'm glad to see you didn't get blown to smithereens.'"

Shredder shook his head. "Sorry, love. I'm afraid life is a bit more complicated than that."

"I know." I didn't really. I couldn't imagine what sort of life he lived that would prevent him from popping in on a friend. I supposed I never would. "Let's move on from October. What's going on with Reggie and Piney that would cause someone like you to come to a place like Rescue?"

"Neither Reggie Slater nor Piney Portman are why I'm here exactly. Although I suppose Reggie played a role."

"Played a role how?"

"Reggie was not only an investment banker but a money launderer who somehow got tied up with the man I'm here to find."

"Money launderer?"

Shredder nodded. "Many of Reggie's investors were wealthy men and women who acquired a large amount of money in an illegal manner and were interested in having it cleaned. These people invested in projects Reggie found for them and were repaid in the form of interest and dividends with money that wouldn't be linked back to the illegal activity associated with the original cash. Reggie was becoming well established and had connections all over the world. According to my sources, he came to Rescue to meet with a man named Deidrick Eckhart, who's a known associate of Valdive Gershwin."

"Deidrick Eckhart…Why do I know that name?"

"You may have met him at the inn."

"Deidrick Eckhart must be the German businessman who was reading in the library on the day Piney died," I said. "Reggie was going to launder money for him?"

"He was. The twist is that Eckhart wasn't Eckhart."

I frowned. "Come again?"

"Let me back up a bit. The organization I work for received intel that Gershwin, who is a money broker of sorts, arranged a deal between Slater and Eckhart."

"Wait." I held up a hand. "What do you mean by money broker?"

"Someone who puts people in possession of illegally acquired money, in this case Eckhart, with people who are willing and able to launder it, in this case Reggie. Gershwin takes a cut of the deal."

"Okay. Go on."

"As I was saying, the organization I work for received intel that Gershwin had set up a deal between Reggie Slater and Deidrick Eckhart. We've been after Gershwin for a long time, so we arranged to have Eckhart detained and one of our operatives came to Rescue pretending to be him. I came along to keep an eye on things. We hoped Reggie would be able to lead us to Gershwin, but as it turned out, he got himself into a dicey situation unrelated to the money deal and our plan fell apart."

"What does this have to do with Reggie's death?"

"I'm not sure. All I know is that Reggie is dead and Trace Rigby, the man masquerading as Eckhart, has disappeared."

"Disappeared?"

"We believe Gershwin figured out what we were doing and kidnapped Rigby. At this point, I'm not even sure whether he's alive or dead. My new mission, which has come about due to my spectacular fail at keeping an eye on Rigby in the first place, is to find him, which is where you come in."

"Me?"

"I'm pretty sure Gershwin is still in the area, I just don't know where. You have contacts, and we both know you have a special gift that helps you find people."

"I'm able to connect with people I'm supposed to rescue," I pointed out. "I doubt I can find some random guy I know very little about."

Shredder's expression softened. "I know your gift has grown beyond simply connecting to rescue victims. I really need you to try. If Rigby is still alive, his life may depend on us finding him before Gershwin decides to cut his losses."

I hesitated.

"I know how this looks. Some man you knew for a few days a year ago shows up for the first time after leaving you in the middle of your own investigation and asks you for a favor. It's downright rude. I get that. But this is important. Rigby is a good guy. He has people who are depending on him to come home. Will you help me?"

I let out a long sigh. "Yeah, I'll help you. But I'm going to need to clear it with Jake. He'll need to find someone to cover my shift at the bar, and he has to know how to reach me in case of a rescue."

"Call him now. I'm sure I can arrange the same consultant's fee I paid you the last time."

Chapter 10

Tuesday, December 18

Shredder showed up the next morning before I'd even had a chance to take the dogs out for their walk. He looked fully awake and ready to tackle the day, while I wanted nothing more than to go back to bed for a couple of hours. With seven dogs needing to go out every morning, I have to be an early riser, but the short days this year were messing with my natural rhythm.

"I have new information," Shredder said upon greeting me.

"The dogs need to go out, so you'll have to talk while we walk," I said, handing Shredder back the jacket he'd just hung on my coatrack.

"That works for me." He greeted an ecstatic Denali, then slipped into the jacket.

I frowned. "Denali has been all gaga over you since you showed up at my place a year ago. You hadn't met him before that, had you?"

"How would I have met him?"

I glanced at Shredder with suspicion in my eyes. "It just doesn't fit that he would adore you on sight. He doesn't trust anyone and greets newcomers with aggression, not doggy kisses."

Shredder shrugged. "Denali is a pack animal. He respects the natural hierarchy that exists between members of the pack and recognizes an alpha when he meets one."

"So you're saying you're the alpha, which is why Denali adores you?"

Shredder shrugged. "Apparently."

I opened the door, and all five house dogs ran out into the frigid darkness. Using my flashlight, I headed to the barn to pick up Juno and Kodi. Shredder's explanation about the alpha male made sense in an odd sort of way, but I wasn't buying that as the entire story. Not only did Denali respect Shredder, he trusted him. There was more to this, but for the life of me, I didn't know what the *more* could be. I'd had Denali for quite a while before I met Shredder, so I didn't see how he could have met my mystery man before last December. Maybe the dog was just a good judge of character and could see into the spirit of a man on his first meeting.

"So what did you find out?" I asked as we got underway. I pointed my flashlight into the distance to make sure the dogs who had taken the lead were still in sight. Normally, Denali, Shia, and Yukon were all up-front, but this morning Denali had chosen to stay back with Shredder, Honey, Lucky, and me.

"Yesterday I shared my belief that it was most likely Gershwin who had Rigby, but since then I've learned that the organization Rigby works for has received a ransom demand from someone named Nicolas Askar, who wants two Turkish spies currently in the custody of the CIA released in exchange for Rigby's life."

"Is the exchange going to be made?"

Shredder shook his head. "No. The deal Askar wants will never fly, but the team is pretending to consider it as a means of stalling. I'm not sure how long Askar will be willing to wait for his demand to be met; I suspect eventually he'll give up and kill Rigby. I have to find Rigby and secure his release before that happens."

"Who exactly is this Askar?" I asked.

"Nicolas Askar, whose real given name is Aslan Askar, is a hired thug who works for whoever is willing to pay his exorbitant fee. We suspect he hooked up with Gershwin because Rigby was in Alaska to find Gershwin and bring him to justice. His request for the release of the two Turks fits because Askar was born in Turkey, although he was educated in France."

"Why there?"

"Askar is intelligent, and his parents had a lot of money. I guess they thought he'd receive a better education in France, so they sent him to boarding school when he was eight. From what I understand, he had a hard time fitting in with his mainly Western European classmates, and he spent a lot of time alone in his room, reading. He became fascinated with Nicholas of Myra, also known as Saint Nicholas. So much so that he took his name."

I paused as the wolves howling in the distance made all the dogs bark. "So you've been assigned to find Rigby, who you believe is being held by Askar, to secure his release before he's killed?"

"In a nutshell."

"So where do we start?" I asked as I stepped over a log.

"I'm not certain where Askar might be holed up at this point. Given the fact that Rigby was taken from Rescue, I'm assuming Askar was also here at one point. I don't know if he is still here, but I hacked into the chief of police's files last night and took a peek at the report pertaining to Reggie's murder. Officer Houston notes there were sleigh tracks found near the body. Askar is known to use a sleigh and reindeer team to get around during the winter, so I thought we'd start by trying to figure out where the sleigh tracks originated. Did you actually see a sleigh?"

Calling Shia and Yukon, I turned back toward the cabin. "No. Neither I nor Houston saw the sleigh. I can't even say for certain a sleigh was in any way involved in Reggie Slater's death. The sleigh tracks we found were accompanied by tracks made by two caribou. We found the same tracks during a rescue on Saturday."

"And the subject and outcome of that rescue?"

I paused to let Lucky catch up. The poor guy had a hard time navigating during the winter even when I'd cleared a path. Perhaps I should have brought the sled. "The subject was an elderly man named Nick who sometimes thinks he's Santa. He'd wandered off from the inn wearing his Santa suit and was found sitting on the inn's front porch with only a vague recollection of how he got there."

"I met Nick Clauston. I wasn't at the inn when he wandered off; I met him the day before. You're saying he didn't remember anything at all about how he got back to the inn?"

"He said he was picked up by Santa, who took him to his reindeer barn and gave him hot cocoa. When he was able to remember where he belonged, the man brought him back. My team thought it odd that if he was found wandering around the man with the sleigh didn't notify the authorities rather than taking him home, but we were so happy Nick was okay, we didn't question things. Do you think the same man who helped Nick killed Reggie?"

"It's possible the man in the sleigh was Askar. It fits in with Askar's infatuation with Saint Nicholas. But we don't have enough to come to any conclusions yet."

I stopped walking and looked around. "If the man with the caribou has been out recently, it would seem we should be able to find tracks to follow. It hasn't snowed much the past twenty-four hours."

"Do you think the dogs can help?" Shredder wondered.

I nodded. "Yukon can track a scent. He might be able to pick up something from the caribou and track it. It's been more than twelve hours since Houston and I found Reggie's body, so the caribou scent will be more than twelve hours old as well. But we can try."

"Let's," Shredder said. "I don't have any better ideas."

Back at the cabin, Shredder helped me feed the animals. Then we leashed both Yukon and Denali and headed out to the place where Houston and I had found Reggie's body. Denali hadn't been trained in search and rescue. Most of the time I didn't bring him along on S&R missions because he wasn't used to following orders, but Shredder thought he had good instincts and was sure he could control the wolf in Denali given their special connection.

I wasn't sure Yukon would understand it was the scent of the caribou and not any of the dozens of other scents that littered the area that I wanted him to track, but after we followed the marks from the sleigh in the snow for a while, it seemed he picked up on the point of our excursion.

"We might be able to backtrack to the beginning of the trip the sleigh took from the tracks in the snow alone," Shredder observed.

"It's fortunate we haven't had snow since we found the body. And the tracks are distinct. It makes me wonder if the person who left the tracks really was the one who killed Reggie. I mean, leaving these tracks wasn't very stealthy."

Shredder frowned. "Yeah, although I suppose the sleigh could just have been driven in the same general area, independent of Reggie's murder."

Shredder and I, Denali and Yukon walked in silence for the next twenty minutes. We followed the tracks, which led deeper into the forest. I could tell we'd headed north, then east. I had a feeling we'd come out not all that far from the inn.

"So are we thinking this Askar killed Reggie?"

"It doesn't make sense he would unless he did it for Gershwin, who might have wanted him dead if Reggie was planning to double-cross him and he found out about it."

I glanced at Yukon, who'd paused to look around. It seemed he sensed something. Then I turned to Denali, who had worked his way around to where Shredder and I were walking. "The dogs sense someone or something. The fact that neither dog is growling indicates to me that they haven't made up their minds about what they sense. It's probably just an animal, but we should keep our eyes open." I tucked my rifle under my armpit so it was ready if I needed it. I was aware that Shredder had a gun tucked into the back of his pants.

He stopped walking and crouched down. "It looks like the tracks lead into the woods to the left. Let's keep the dogs close. We may even want to leash them. I have a feeling we're getting close."

As Shredder suggested, we put both dogs on leashes. We wanted to be able to sneak up on the house from which the sleigh tracks began when we finally found it. Shredder seemed to have an idea how to proceed, so I let him make the decisions and simply followed. After we'd walked as quietly as possible for a good twenty minutes, a large white ranch house with an old barn and rail corral came into view.

"Looks promising," Shredder said. "Wait here with the dogs. I'm going to sneak around through the forest and approach from the barn side."

"Do you think we should call for backup? For Houston?" I said.

"For all we know, we'll find a family getting ready for lunch. I'll do some recon and we can figure out what to do next after that." Shredder reached down and scrubbed both dogs necks with his large hands. "I won't be long. Stay out of sight and keep the dogs quiet."

I can't express how much I hate waiting. Waiting is for the timid and passive. It isn't a behavior I enjoy. I glanced down at the dogs. I didn't have a lot of choice. If I tied them up and left them here, they'd have a fit, and if there was someone in the house, they'd hear them for sure. I could try following Shredder with the dogs, but the last thing I wanted to do was put them in danger. In hindsight, we might have been better off leaving them at home, but they were the type of dogs who were good to have on hand in a crisis. Bringing them had made sense.

I had no idea where Shredder was as he made his way around the perimeter. It wasn't until he ran across the clearing behind the barn that I had some sense of what he might do next. I could feel my heart race as I clamped down on both leashes. The next few minutes were going to be critical. Not knowing what to expect was a lot worse than knowing what was coming, even if what was to come was dangerous or unpleasant.

The minutes clicked slowly by. Where was he? It seemed to me he'd had plenty of time to peek in through a few windows and assess the situation. Just about the time I was ready to head to the house despite his order to stay put, I saw him emerge from the front door. He waved in my direction, indicating it was okay to come forward. Hanging on to both dogs, who had begun to whine when they'd seen Shredder, I took a step toward the house. Hopefully, he didn't have a gun to his back and the dogs and I weren't walking into a trap.

Holding my breath for at least the first ten steps, I began to relax when no one shot at us. Some part of me knew Shredder wouldn't have waved us forward if doing so would put us in danger, even if he did have a gun to his back.

"The place is empty?" I asked as I arrived at the front porch.

"Totally. There are signs that reindeer have been here as recently as this morning, but there's no sign of the animals or the sleigh now."

"What now?"

Shredder scanned the area. "I have a feeling that..." His phone pinged and he pulled it from his pocket. He frowned.

"What is it?" I asked.

"Facial recognition scans placed Askar in Tinseltown this morning."

"Facial recognition scans?"

"Basically the software looks for a match to an image you provide. The software can scan thousands of photos a minute that make their way into databases via social media, traffic cams, etc." Shredder passed me the phone which featured a photo. "This is Askar and the photo of him standing in front of the Santa House in Tinseltown was posted to an Instagram account this morning."

I looked at the photo. He looked to be an elderly man with a long face and a gray beard. His sharp features were accentuated by his stern expression. He was tall and thin, with an almost regal air about him. As Shredder had said, he was standing in front of the Santa house in the small town of Tinseltown, Alaska. He didn't appear to be posing; it was as if he wasn't aware his photo was being snapped. I imagined the photo was taken by a tourist, and Askar just happened to step in front of the intended object.

"Your people sent the photo to you?"

Shredder took the phone back. "Yes. It looks like I'm heading to Tinseltown."

"I'm coming with you. Now that you got me in to this, I want to see it through."

"I suppose your unique gift could come in handy. Perhaps we should bring Yukon as well. If we can find something with Askar's scent, he might be able to help us track him down. We'll most likely need to stay over at least one night. You aren't expected to go in to work today, which just leaves your animals. The last time I was here, a friend helped you out. Is there someone who can help out with the animals now?"

"Once you confirm your directive is to head to Tinseltown, I'll make some calls to line someone up."

The last time Shredder took me off on a wild-goose chase, Justine, the receptionist at the veterinary clinic, pet sat for me overnight. I was sure she'd do it again, but so would Chloe, and Serena would do it as well. Chloe would ask a lot of questions I wasn't prepared to answer, though, while Serena would help out minus the interrogation, so I decided to give her a call. As I'd anticipated, she was fine with staying at the cabin while I was away "training." All the animals knew her, but I was worried Denali would give her a hard time, so if the trip was going to happen, I'd drop him off with Jake. It would lead to questions, but it was the best option I had.

Chapter 11

"Are you sure about this?" Jake asked two hours later when I left Denali at his house. "This could be dangerous, and Shredder is a spy, while you're a civilian. What does he need you for anyway?"

"He probably doesn't need me, but I want to go. I know you'll worry, but I'll be fine. You can trust me and you can trust Shredder. I might be back tomorrow, but it'll more likely be Thursday."

Jake ran his hand through his thick hair. "I want you to call me to check in. Every day. More than once a day. Every few hours wouldn't be asking too much."

I put my hands on my hips and looked at him. "Would you be this worried if it was one of the guys going to Tinseltown to help Shredder?"

"No. But you aren't one of the guys. You're family. The only family I have. I can't help but worry about you."

I felt my face soften. "I know. And I'll be careful and call you so often, you'll be irritated by all the calls." I reached down and ruffled Denali's ears. "Yukon is coming with me and Denali will be fine with you. The others will be fine with Serena, but do you think you could check on her? You never know when Homer is going to decide to be stubborn or Moose will hide and make you look for him."

Jake gave me a tight hug. "I'll check on your babies. If you need anything, anything at all, don't hesitate to call me."

I leaned my head on his chest and listened to his heartbeat for a moment. He really was my rock. The one person I depended on above all others. "Try not to worry."

After I left Jake's, I drove to Harley's to check on Brando, who was settling in just fine. Harley was getting the hang of letting the pup know who was boss, but of course Harley being Harley, he was a sweet, cuddly alpha, not all sharp and mysterious like Shredder. I made up an excuse about search-and-rescue training to explain my absence for a few days if I didn't make it back to check on them, then went home to pack. I wouldn't need much—a change of clothes, toiletries, maybe a second pair of boots in case the first got wet. I doubted we'd be going out for any fancy dinners, so I was pretty sure jeans and sweaters would be fine throughout. The last time Shredder and I had headed out on a fact-finding trip our reservation had gotten messed up and we'd ended up sharing a room. Two beds, but still one room. Something nonrevealing to sleep in seemed like a good idea just in case, so I added it to my mental list.

By the time I arrived at my cabin Shredder was waiting. It looked like he'd brought all his luggage, not just an overnight bag.

"I thought this was just a quick trip?"

"I checked out of the inn. There isn't a reason for me to be there any longer now that my cover has been blown. It looked as if Reggie's friends were planning to take off as well. In fact, the inn was pretty deserted. I feel bad for the owners, but maybe they can rent my room to someone else for the holiday."

"I hope so. It must be pretty depressing to go from having ten rooms rented to none at all. I'm assuming Mr. Clauston and his daughter and son-in-law have already left?"

Shredder nodded. "I paid for my unused nights. I'm not sure what the others did. Are you ready?"

"Give me ten minutes to pack and grab some supplies for Yukon and we can be on our way. I guess we're taking your rental?"

"We are. Your Jeep looks like it could break down before we even hit the town limits."

I shrugged. "It's an old Jeep, but it's all I have. I can't afford a new one, so Jake keeps patching it up. Do you have an emergency survival kit?"

"Always."

******

Tinseltown was a small town located to the southeast of Fairbanks, literally built to support its name by ensuring that every aspect of it was dedicated to the idea of a Santa's village. Not only were many of the lampposts wrapped in red and white to look like candy canes, but most of the streets had

Christmassy names. While it made one feel as if they'd been transported to a real Santa's village three hundred and sixty five days a year, during the Christmas season it was truly magical.

"It looks like everyone's having a good time," Shredder said as he carefully navigated the crowded streets, where masses of people spilled from the sidewalks into the roads.

"I enjoy the festive feeling in the air." I turned and glanced at Shredder. "I know your facial recognition program put Askar in town this morning, but do you think he's still here?"

"I have no idea. Given what I know of him, he might be interested in the Santa festival, but if he has Rigby, I doubt he'd be spending time at events."

"Maybe he's here for some other reason altogether," I suggested.

"Perhaps."

"Rigby was kidnapped in Rescue, but it makes sense he'd move him to another location. Tinseltown is near enough that Askar wasn't moving him all that far, but far enough away that he wouldn't have been easily discovered if not for the photo."

Shredder didn't respond. From the expression on his face, he must be deep in thought.

I pointed into the distance. "I think the hotel you booked us into is down that street. You did book us *rooms*, right? As in two?"

"I booked a suite. Two bedrooms plus a sitting area where we can eat and work if we need to. Just so you know, we're booked as Chris and Claudia Stone."

"Chris and Claudia?"

"I was in a hurry, and Chris is a name I've used before."

"You'll need ID to check in. I don't suppose you have ID with the name Chris Stone on it?"

Shredder smiled at me. "Yes. As I said, it's a name I've used before."

"And you told them about Yukon?"

"I did, and while they don't usually allow pets, they were fine with having a service dog on the premises."

I sat back and tried to enjoy the hustle and bustle of the busy streets as I pondered what it must be like to be Shredder. To have different names you'd need to remember all the time. To travel so often you never had anywhere to call home. To put yourself in danger day after day to protect or rescue people you didn't know and may never meet. I supposed in a way, the search-and-rescue team put themselves in danger for people they didn't know on a regular basis, but somehow Shredder's life seemed so lonely and empty.

The rustic inn at the end of a dead-end street provided for a quiet location even though it was just a block from the activity of the festive little town square. The room featured a white brick fireplace that was framed by two white sofas and a dark mahogany coffee table. Behind the sofas was a dining table made from the same wood, a minibar, and a small kitchenette. On either side of the living area was a large bedroom with its own bath. Shredder let me choose the room I wanted and I went with the one that overlooked the snow-covered forest in the back.

Yukon walked around the room, sniffing everything, while I set my overnight bag on the white bedspread with a red-and-black-plaid comforter folded over the foot. Matching throw pillows made the room feel very Christmassy, although not as much as the main room, which boasted not only a six-foot tree but an arrangement of pine-cone garlands on the mantel as well. I could hear Shredder moving around in his room and decided to take a minute to wash up before we went out. It seemed it had already been such a long day, and I was exhausted.

To make good on my promise to call Jake often, I called him to let him know we'd arrived.

"I take it you made it safely?" Jake said on answering.

"We did. The inn is lovely and the town is so charming that for a minute, I totally forgot we were here to find a man who's been taken hostage, not to find the holiday spirit. How's Denali doing? He isn't big on change."

"He's okay. Houston stopped by with Kojak and the dogs are playing while we share a couple of beers."

"You didn't tell him about Shredder?"

"No. I didn't say anything he didn't already know. If you ask me, you should tell him everything when you get back. You and Houston have a good partnership going. You don't want to mess it up with secrets that wouldn't reveal anything much anyway."

"What do you mean?"

"What's the harm in telling Houston you have a friend named Shredder who works for some highly classified government agency and are helping him on a project? That's really all you know, and it doesn't expose anything because Shredder isn't the guy's real name anyway."

Jake had a point. "I'll think about it. I need to go now. I'll call you later."

I hung up and headed out to the common area, where Shredder was working on his computer. Yukon followed me and, after giving this room a good sniff too, settled down on the rug in front of the fire. "I'm ready to go out whenever you are."

"I got a schedule of events from the front desk. Apparently, there's a party for the Santa impersonators and their elves tonight. I thought we'd go and ask around about Askar. Maybe someone has seen him or knows where we can find him."

"But we don't have costumes," I said.

Someone knocked, and Shredder gestured toward the door. "We do now."

I groaned as I crossed the room and opened the door to find a woman dressed in a tiny elf costume holding two dress bags. I took them and thanked her. I closed the door, turned, and looked at Shredder. "Please tell me I'm going as Santa and you're the elf."

Shredder chuckled. "I would have divided things in that manner if it would have made you feel more comfortable, but they didn't have an elf costume in my size. As it is, I had to guess at yours. Hopefully, it will fit. The costume shop didn't have much of a selection left."

I opened the bag and pulled out a tiny red and green elf suit. "So you and I are going to party dressed in these very authentic-looking costumes?"

"That's the idea. We have an hour to get ready."

I looked at the very short red skirt, which I figured out was supposed to cover green tights. This couldn't get much worse.

******

The party was amazing. I'm not sure if I'd say it was good amazing or bad, but it definitely was amazing. Everyone had gotten into the spirit of the event and the room was filled with Santas and elves in red and green outfits. Some, like mine, were ridiculously skimpy, while other elves wore green pants and long-sleeved red shirts with green suspenders. What I wouldn't give for a pair of pants and a long-sleeved shirt.

Maybe I could find someone to trade with. When we'd first arrived and I'd seen the elves in pants, I'd asked Shredder why I couldn't have had a costume with pants. He claimed the costume shop was out of elf costumes with pants, but I suspected he was lying. If I found out for certain he was, I can guarantee you that he was going to suffer.

"Your costume is so cute," said another elf in an equally skimpy costume. "My name is Tammy. Tammy Winters."

I opened my mouth to reply, but for the life of me, I couldn't remember my fake name. "I'm happy to meet you. Your costume is great."

"I love dressing up and this event is the best. Don't you think so?"

"It's really something."

Tammy grinned. "This is my fifth year attending. Last year I was awarded the runner-up ribbon for best costume. I hoped to have time to really go all-out and compete for the top prize, but my boss turned into a real Scrooge and wouldn't give me the time off I needed to properly prepare." Tammy put her arms out to the side. "Still, I think this costume came out okay."

I raised a brow. I had to admit Tammy had assets that allowed her costume to fill out a lot more fully than mine. She looked more like a Playboy Bunny elf. There was no doubt in my mind that if the judges were male, she'd be the winner.

"Are you here with a date?" Tammy asked.

I nodded. "Yes, I'm with one of these Santas." I had to laugh at the absurdity of that statement as I looked around the room for Shredder. "I don't see him right now, but with all the beards and fake bellies, they look sort of alike. Unlike the elves." My eyes couldn't help but drop to Tammy's ample breasts, which looked as if they were going to pop out of her tight-fitting top. "Are you here with someone?"

"No. I mean yes. Well, actually, no."

"I see."

"It's just my boyfriend, Tommy, is an ass."

Tommy and Tammy: how cute. Or not. "An ass?"

"I know that isn't nice to say, but he is," Tammy continued. "He wasn't here for two minutes and he was already panting around after the lollipop elf."

"The lollipop elf?" I asked.

Tammy pointed across the room where an elf dressed in pink with a lollipop hat was rubbing her own ample assets against a tall and oddly thin Santa.

"Is the Santa she's doing the mating dance with Tommy?" I asked.

Tammy balled up her fists. "It is. I'm so darn close to hauling off and decking her, it isn't even funny. But Tommy would like that. Two women fighting over him would stroke his giant ego, which, trust me, doesn't need to be stroked." Tammy looked around the room. "No. I need to fight fire with fire." She smiled. "And I know just how to do it."

Chapter 12

I watched as Tammy sauntered across the room to where a shirtless Santa wearing pants with suspenders and a fireman's hat was pounding down shots like there was no tomorrow. Seriously? Geez, I needed to get out of here. I looked around for Shredder but didn't see him right off. I was sure he was somewhere among the masses, but it felt like more effort than it was worth to make the rounds looking for him. I decided to try to find my jacket and then go outside for some fresh air. I was sorting through the jackets that were piled one atop another when I noticed Tammy leaving with her fireman Santa. I wasn't sure he'd end up being any better than Tommy, but it wasn't my place to have an opinion.

"I don't suppose you have a smoke you can spare?" a Santa dressed like a cowboy asked when I'd made my way outdoors.

"I'm sorry, I don't smoke. I just came out for some fresh air," I replied.

The Santa stared at my green legs, which showed below the hem of my jacket. "Just as well. I'm trying to quit," he said, holding out a hand.

I did the polite thing and shook it. When he lingered, I gave him a look that almost made him yelp.

"Is this your first year at the event?" Cowboy Santa asked.

"It is. I came to meet up with a friend, but I haven't been able to find him. I don't suppose you've seen a tall, thin, regal-looking Santa with darkish skin, a real gray beard, and a foreign accent?" I assumed Nicolas spoke with an accent, though I didn't know that for a fact. "His real name is Nicolas, but I forgot to ask him if he uses a different name for events."

"I know Nicolas, but I haven't seen him this year. He's been a regular in the past, so I imagine he's around somewhere."

"Damn," I said. "I really wanted to see him. I don't suppose you know where he usually stays?"

He shook his head. "Sorry. I'm pretty sure he rents a house outside town. I'm not sure of the address, but you might ask Queenie."

"Queenie?"

"The head elf. She's the one who organizes this event. You would have met her when you signed up."

"Oh, of course." I hit the side of my head, like I was somehow losing my marbles. "Queenie. How could I forget? I'm not sure I remember seeing her this evening."

"She's around. She's dressed like a Little Red Riding Hood elf. You can't miss the long red cape."

I sent him the biggest smile I could muster up. "I appreciate the information, but it's freezing out here. I'm heading in."

Hopefully, I'd find this Queenie and she would know where we could find Nicolas and this crazy mission Shredder had dragged me in to would be over almost before it began. Lord, I wanted to go home to my little cabin and my animals.

The heat in the building felt stifling after the frigid air outside. I took off my jacket, tossed it on the pile, and went in search of Shredder. I was halfway across the room and heading to the bar when the Santa Tammy had pointed out as being her date, Tommy, grabbed my arm and pulled me aside.

I stomped on his foot.

"Ouch, that hurt." He let go of my arm.

I puffed out a breath. "If you grab me again, you're going to find out what real hurt is. What do you want?"

He leaned over and tried rubbing his foot through his black Santa boot, which was ridiculous. "I'm looking for Tammy. I saw you talking to her earlier. Do you know where she is?"

I narrowed my eyes. I wasn't sure I wanted to get in the middle of whatever drama was going on between Tammy and Tommy, so I chose a simple answer. "She left."

"Left? But how? She came with me so she doesn't have a car." He held out the red fuzzy gloves I just realized he was holding. "She didn't even take her mittens."

"Look, I'm sure she's fine. She was angry you were talking to the lollipop elf, so she…" I gasped as an image flashed through my mind.

"Are you okay?" he asked.

I put a hand to my chest. "It's Tammy. I think she might be in trouble."

"Trouble?" His voice rose two octaves. "What kind of trouble?"

I looked him in the eye. "I came here with a man dressed as a regular Santa. We need to find him. Right away."

"What's his name?"

"Um?" Dang it, what was his name? "Chris. His name is Chris. Chris Stone. I'm going to sit down at that booth. Find Chris and bring him to me, and while you're looking for Chris, I'll try to figure out where Tammy is."

"Figure out? How are you going to do that? How do you know she's in trouble?"

I grabbed Tommy by the shoulders and looked him in the eye. "You're wasting time. Find Chris!"

I grabbed the gloves and headed to the booth. Holding the gloves, I closed my eyes. I could sense Tammy. She was cold. And frightened. No, not frightened: terrified.

It's okay, I thought, on the off chance I could make a two-way connection. I was less than twenty percent in my ability to make them, but sometimes ...

Tammy looked around. "Who's there?"

It's me. The elf you spoke to about Tommy, before you left with the fireman Santa. I want to help you, but I need you to stay calm.

I could sense Tammy's anxiety growing, but also a willingness to let me in. That was good. And rare, although I supposed my power had been growing rapidly of late.

I can sense you're cold and scared. I can see darkness around you, but not much else. I need you to help me know where you are.

Tammy looked around frantically. "Where are you? I can hear you, but I can't see you."

I focused as hard as I could so I didn't lose her. *I'm not there. Not physically. I'm in your head. I'll explain later, but right now I need you to trust me.*

Tammy sat down on the hard ground and put her head on her upturned knees. She began to sob. I could feel her beginning to fade.

Tammy. I need you to listen. Tommy's here. He's sorry for talking to the lollipop elf. He wants to make it up to you, but first we need to find you. We need you to help us do that.

Tammy lifted her head. "Tommy? Tommy's there?"

Yes.

"Prove it. Ask him what our song is."

I looked around the room for Tommy, who, fortunately, was on his way across the room with Shredder. "What's your and Tammy's song?" I asked as soon as he reached me.

"Huh? What does that have to do with anything?"

"Just tell me."

"'Baby, It's Cold Outside.'"

I closed my eyes and focused. *"Baby, It's Cold Outside."*

"Yes," Tammy sobbed. "That's it."

Okay, now you need to help me. Do you know where you are?

"I'm in the forest. I'm not sure where. I left the bar with the asshole fireman and he suggested we go to his house. He had a car, and I was mad at Tommy, so I went, but instead of going to his house, he drove to a deserted road and parked. He got real handsy real fast. And he was kind of mean. I told him I changed my mind and wanted to go back to the party, but he wouldn't take me. He told me to take my jacket off. When I wouldn't, he slapped me and began ripping at my clothes. I knew he was going to rape me, so I waited for him to be distracted, then I opened the car door, got out, and ran."

I could sense Tammy was beginning to lose feeling in her feet. We needed to find her fast.

"I know that was dumb. I have no idea where I am or how to get back to town. You have to help me."

I will. I need you to stay with me. Find a place to wait. Is there anything you can use to help you stay warm?

"I don't know. Like what?"

Anything will help. Even tree branches.

"I'll look around."

Okay, do that. I'm coming for you, but I'm not sure how long it will take. Is there anything at all you can remember about the drive in the car? Anything that might help me focus on a location?

"I know we drove north on the main highway for maybe five minutes before turning off onto a side road. There was a sign for the festival where we turned. Then we drove a few more minutes."

Okay, good. That helps. Find the warmest place you can to wait and then stay put. I'll be there as soon as I can.

I hated to break the connection, but I was going to need help. I opened my eyes to find Shredder trying to convince Tommy I wasn't crazy. "We need to get Yukon and we need to call the police. We need help."

"We can't call the police," Tommy said. "Tammy is on probation. She isn't even supposed to be in Alaska, but we come here every year and hated to miss it, so we figured a few days wouldn't hurt. If we call the cops, she'll be arrested for breaking probation. Let's see if she's where I think she is. If not, we'll call the cops then."

"If we don't find her, she'll die," I said.

"Maybe we can find her. The three of us," Tommy persisted.

I glanced at Shredder. "It's your call, love," he said.

"Okay," I said. "Let's grab Yukon and head to the spot Tammy described. If we don't find her right away, we call the cops."

"Okay," Tommy agreed.

The three of us piled into Shredder's car. We stopped at the inn to get Yukon and then followed the directions Tammy had given me. Luckily, there had been a light dusting of snow, so once we pulled off the highway onto the narrow local road just after the festival sign, there was a single set of tire tracks to follow. After a few minutes we found the spot where the fireman Santa must have pulled off the road. Shredder parked and we all got out.

I used the gloves to give Yukon the scent. "This is Tammy. We need to find Tammy. Find Tammy, Yukon, find Tammy."

Yukon sniffed the gloves, then began sniffing the ground. Shredder and Tommy used flashlights to look for Tammy's footprints. I could still sense her, but she was no longer responding to my attempts to connect with her. We were running out of time. I'd give it five minutes; if we hadn't found her by then, I was calling the police.

It took Yukon only a few minutes before he alerted. I could see he had the scent and, hopefully, the path Tammy had taken. "Find Tammy," I said again.

Yukon took off through the dense forest. The route Tammy seemed to have taken was pretty random, even crossing itself a few times, but it took Yukon only a few minutes more to find the frightened elf, who had managed to find enough branches to sit on and wrap herself up in. That extra warmth probably made the difference in finding Tammy cold but unharmed and finding her dead.

"The branches worked." Tammy flung her arms around my neck and sobbed. "I was so cold and so scared."

"You're fine now. Let's get you back to your hotel."

Poor Tammy was suffering from mild frostbite, and the prickling sensation she would endure as she thawed out wouldn't be pleasant, but I didn't think she'd suffer any long-term harm from her experience. As soon as we reached the motel where they were staying, I told Tommy to draw Tammy a warm but not hot bath.

"I don't suppose you have a photo of the man who brought you out here?" Shredder asked while Tommy went to do it.

"I do." Tammy held up her phone. "I took a selfie of us before I realized he was a psycho."

Shredder held out his hand. Tammy passed him the phone. He forwarded the photo to his own phone.

"I understand your being in Alaska puts you in violation of your probation," Shredder said.

Tammy hung her head. "I'm not supposed to leave California."

"I'm going to suggest you return to California right away. Send me proof that you're there by the end of the day tomorrow and I won't turn you in to your probation officer."

"Okay," Tammy agreed. "I'll book us on the next flight out of here. And thank you." Tammy looked at Shredder and then at me. "Both of you." Tammy looked at Yukon. "And thank you too, you beautiful dog."

When the bath was run, I tested the temperature, then instructed Tammy to let her body heat up slowly. I hugged her once more, and then Shredder and I headed to the car. It wasn't far to the place where we were staying, which was good, because I was more than ready to settle in for the night.

"Well that was an interesting evening," I said after I changed into my flannel pajamas and pulled a long, warm robe on top.

"I'm glad we got to Tammy in time and that we were able to contain the situation. It wouldn't have helped our search for Nicolas if everyone started talking about the girl with psychic abilities."

"About that: I may have a lead. A Santa dressed as a cowboy told me that he knew a man named Nicolas who fits your man's description. He hadn't seen him this year, but he's a regular visitor to this festival, and when he's here, he usually rents a place outside town."

"Did he have an address or give you directions?"

I shook my head. "He didn't know exactly where the house was, but Queenie might." I gave Shredder as much information about her as I knew.

Shredder looked at his watch. "The event will be over now. We'll pick up on this tomorrow."

I yawned. "Do you think we can find him?"

Shredder nodded. "I do. I just hope we find him in time to save Rigby's life."

Chapter 13

Wednesday, December 19

Shredder knocked on my door early the next morning. I was used to getting up early because I had the dogs to walk and the other animals to tend to, but I swear, when he knocked, it felt like I'd just gotten to sleep. Groaning loudly, I rolled out of bed and greeted Yukon who thumped his tail on the carpeted floor. Pulling on my robe, I called to him and wandered into the common area, where Shredder had a pot of coffee and a tray of warm muffins waiting.

"What time is it?" I yawned.

"Seven o'clock."

"That late? It feels like the middle of the night." I sat down in a chair in front of the fire with the coffee Shredder had handed me.

"I'm sure channeling a person in trouble is very taxing, and you didn't have Moose to help you come down from this one."

That was true, though I was surprised Shredder knew it. Yes, he'd been around me during a rescue before, and yes, I'd explained how Moose helped to keep me sane, but he'd only been in my life for a few days before he disappeared as abruptly as he'd appeared last year, so I was surprised he remembered.

"Do we have a plan for the day?" I asked as I let the coffee slowly pull me into the land of the living.

"I thought we'd get something more to eat, then look around for Queenie. I asked about her at the front desk and they had a phone number for her, but it just rings and rings. It doesn't even go to voice mail. That didn't seem to surprise the woman at the desk. It seems Queenie is quite the character, and she wouldn't be surprised if she was antivoice mail, but she thought we'd find her in town at one of the Santa events. She just didn't know which one."

I leaned back in the chair and put my feet up on the footrest. "Do we know what events are scheduled for this morning?"

"There's a breakfast with Santa that's a fundraiser for the children's hospital, and a toy show and contest that will be taking place in Santa's Workshop all day."

"What's the toy contest about?"

"The entrants present original handmade toys. It sounds like people come from all over the country, even from around the world to enter, because it's common for representatives from toy companies to be in attendance as well."

I put my hand over my mouth to stifle another yawn. "Anything else?"

"Today's the meet and greet for the Elf pageant."

"Elf pageant?"

"It's like a beauty pageant, but the best elf is chosen based on contests each entrant competes in. The audience votes, and today is the meet and greet, where anyone who wishes can speak to their favorite elves and ask them questions."

It sounded like a little slice of hell, but who was I to judge? "It sounds like we're in for an interesting morning if we don't find Queenie on the first try. I assume we're starting with the breakfast."

"That was my plan. The doors open at eight, so we'd best get going. I'll take Yukon out for a walk, then feed him while you get ready. I guess we should just leave him here and come back for him after we find Queenie and hopefully find out where Askar usually stays."

I drank the rest of my coffee and pulled myself out of the chair. I hoped I wasn't coming down with something. I felt like I was 120 today. If I was getting sick, I was going to blame Shredder for making me wear that ridiculous elf costume, which did absolutely zero to protect a person from the elements on a cold winter night.

******

I expected the breakfast with Santa to be lame and corny, but when I saw the faces of the children who were lucky enough to attend, I realized it was charming bordering on magical. Every little girl and boy in the room had a huge grin on their face as they ate pancakes, drank hot cocoa, and listened to stories read by an elf as Santa sat on his throne in preparation for the photos that would be taken after the meal. If I was the one organizing this thing, I'd have done the photos first; it appeared more than one little cherub had hot cocoa spilled down the front of their shirt or dress. But perhaps the spills and imperfect outfits were part of the charm of having breakfast with Santa.

The food smelled wonderful and I wished we had time to stay, but Shredder was able to ascertain within a few minutes that, while Queenie had been there during the setup for the event, she'd turned monitoring duties over to her assistant elf and gone on to other things once the guests arrived. The elf Shredder spoke to suspected the toy show and contest was next on Queenie's agenda, so that was where we set out for next.

Like the breakfast room, Santa's Toy Shop had been decorated to bring out the wonder in everyone who visited, no matter their age. The walls and furniture were painted in bright colors and cheery carols played in the background. Long tables had been set up for those who'd entered their toys to display them. I noticed a wide range of items, from simple hand-carved trucks, trains, and tractors to video games and realistic-looking robots. The elf in charge of the toy shop also informed us that Queenie had been and gone. It seemed you had to get up pretty early in the morning to catch up with the dynamo who organized and managed this entire event.

"See that Santa over there by the trains?" I said to Shredder.

He looked in the direction I was pointing. "What about him?"

"He's dressed in traditional Santa garb this morning, but I'm ninety percent sure he's the fireman Santa Tammy left with last night. The one who tried to rape her."

Shredder frowned. "I'm going to make a call. Wait here and keep an eye on him. Whatever you do, don't approach him or engage with him in any way. Just keep him in your sights."

"Okay," I said as Shredder walked away. I saw him pull out his phone, and he was engaged in a conversation before he'd even made it out of the building. Less than five minutes later, he returned to where I was waiting. Fireman Santa hadn't moved.

"I've spoken to a contact who's notified the local authorities. There are people on the way. We'll wait here until they arrive."

"Can they arrest him on our word alone?"

"Probably not, but I didn't make the call myself. I had someone from the FBI do it, claiming a call came in from an anonymous source. The person my contact spoke to told him there were two other women who'd been raped by a man dressed as Santa in the past week. They have the rapist's DNA from one of the other victims, so if he's the guy, they'll be able to prove it. At the very least, they'll detain and test him."

Shredder and I watched as two uniformed officers came into the building, made their way across the room, and pulled the Santa I'd fingered aside. They spoke to him for several minutes before one of them pulled out his cuffs and secured the guy. We watched as the officers led him out of the building.

"Looks like local law enforcement has things under control. We can be on our way."

"Yeah," I said as I watched the crowd fill in after the men left. "That's a good idea."

Although we continued our search, we didn't find Queenie at the bakeshop, the elf library, or the candy cane factory. We finally caught up with her at the ice-skating rink on the edge of the park.

"You're looking for Nicolas? Do you mind if I ask why?" the feisty little woman demanded.

"We just want to speak to him about a friend of ours," Shredder replied. "We were at the Santa meet and greet last night, and a few of the folks we talked to thought Nicolas might be able to help put us in touch with him."

Queenie shrugged. "I guess it won't hurt to give you directions to his friend's place. If you aren't supposed to be there, you'll be stopped at the gate."

Shredder smiled. "Thank you so much for your help."

When Shredder and I went back to our suite, he unlocked the metal suitcase he'd been carting around and took out guns of varying types and sizes that he began tucking into pockets and his waistband. I realized very quickly that the charming, enchanted part of our day had come to an end and things were about to get very real.

******

"Do you think Rigby is still alive?" I asked as we sped down the icy road.

Shredder let out a long, slow breath. "I have no idea. If he is still alive, we're running out of time. I'm hoping we'll find him today."

I thought about the family who was hoping and praying for his safe return and said a little prayer of my own that we'd find and rescue him in time. There was nothing worse than waiting on the sidelines to find out whether the person you cared about most in the world was going to live or die.

"Queenie mentioned the place having a guard," I said. "There are just two of us. Do you have a plan to get in and then, even more importantly, get out again?"

"Not yet," Shredder admitted.

When we were about a half mile from the property, Shredder pulled off the road. He found a place to tuck the vehicle in behind a thick grove of evergreens and told me to wait while he checked out the situation. He returned after what seemed like a lifetime.

"It looks deserted except for the man at the gate," he informed me.

"What do you mean, deserted?"

"I mean I spent a good amount of time checking the place out and as far as I can tell, there isn't anyone on the property other than the guard at the gate. That doesn't mean Rigby isn't inside. We'll just need to tread lightly."

"What do you want me to do?"

Shredder chewed on his bottom lip, appearing to consider the situation.

"Did you bring your elf costume as I asked?"

I groaned. "Yeah, I brought it."

"Put it on. You're going to pretend your car broke down on your way to the festival. I'm hoping you'll distract the guard while I go over the wall and find a way into the house. If I find Rigby, I'll need another distraction to get us out, so maybe you can convince him to let you wait inside the gatehouse with him until the tow truck arrives."

"Okay," I agreed. "I'll play the helpless elf, but you owe me."

Shredder pulled the car onto the road and disabled it in case the guard decided to check out my story. Then he took off through the woods toward the house, while I changed into my elf costume. With the red and green monstrosity in place, I got out of the car and walked down the road to the gate. By the time I got there, I was freezing, so I hoped for more reasons than one that the guard would let me wait in the gatehouse with him."

"Can I help you, miss?" the guard asked as I walked up to the gatehouse.

"I hope so." I offered him my biggest smile. "I was on my way to the Santa Festival when my car broke down. I called for a tow truck, but the man said he's busy and can't be here for at least an hour. The engine won't start, so I can't run the heater and I'm freezing. I don't suppose you'd let me wait in the house?"

He looked toward the large building. "No one's home right now, but I suppose I can let you wait in here with me."

I let out a sigh that seemed to freeze in the frigid air. "Thank you so much. I'm afraid this costume doesn't offer a lot of protection against the elements."

I settled onto a stool and began to ask him questions about the town and the festival. It appeared I had his full attention, which was good, because the camera happened to catch Shredder going over the wall. Fortunately, the guard was looking at my cleavage and not the monitors then. When I saw Shredder head toward the back of the large house, I launched into a hilarious story that should have earned me an acting award. I hoped it was funny enough to keep the man's interest until Shredder got inside.

After a few minutes, I saw a shadow on the monitor that showed the kitchen. If no one was home, as the guard claimed, I had to assume Shredder had made it inside and the shadow belonged to him. I hoped he'd hurry up and get out of there; to be honest, I'm not that naturally charming. Keeping the guard from checking the monitors for much longer wasn't going to be easy, and I wondered whether Shredder realized there were cameras focused on the house; he'd shown up on screens two more times.

Just then, the guard turned around and glanced at the screens.

"I don't suppose you have a bathroom I could use? I really, really need to go." I wiggled around just enough to sell it, I hoped.

He turned back to me, looking uncertain. "I probably shouldn't let anyone inside."

"I get that, but I really have to go. You can come with me if you'd feel better about it."

"I guess it wouldn't hurt to let you use the bathroom on the first floor."

I said how very appreciative I was as he grabbed his jacket. He glanced at the way I was dressed and offered it to me. "You need this more than I do."

I gasped as Shredder's image flashed across the screen. Luckily, the guard was still looking at me.

"Are you okay?" he asked.

"I'm fine," I answered. "My stomach is just a little rumbly."

"We'd better hurry." He opened the gatehouse door and gestured for me to precede him. Now I just had to hope we wouldn't run into Shredder while we were in the house. Using the bathroom might not have been the best idea, but it was the only thing I could think of to get the guard away from the monitors.

I stalled as long as I could in the bathroom before the guard and I started back to the gatehouse. I hoped Shredder was almost done inside; I was running out of ideas to distract the guard. Just as we entered the gatehouse, I got a text from Shredder, letting me know he was clear.

"Problem?" the guard asked as I looked at the phone.

"It's the tow truck driver. He's going to be another hour. Maybe I should just text a friend to pick me up and worry about the car later."

"Might be a good idea."

I texted Shredder to come pick me up. When he honked the horn a short while later, the guard seemed to buy that Shredder was the friend I'd texted and didn't ask any questions. He was probably too happy to get rid of me to care.

"I take it you didn't find Rigby?" I asked when Shredder and I were on our way.

"He wasn't in the house. I suspected as much when I realized there was only one guard, but I needed to be sure."

"Did you know there were security cameras in practically every room? I almost died when I saw you flash across the screen."

"Damn. They must have a double-blind system."

"Double-blind?"

"One set of cameras in plain sight, which I avoided, but there must be a second set that's hidden. I should have known. I feel like I'm really off my game lately. First Rigby gets nabbed right out from under me, and then I fall for the double-blind thing."

"Having cameras in plain sight make good camouflage for hidden cameras. I'd never think to look for a second set of cameras. It's genius really."

"It's a common enough strategy I shouldn't have been fooled by. I'll need to be more careful in the future."

"Did you find anything that could help us at all?" I asked.

"Maybe. There were men's clothes in the closet of one of the guest rooms in a size I imagine would fit Askar. And there was an address jotted down on a notepad next to the landline, and a copy of an email on the nightstand with instructions to the Santa parade that's held at three o'clock this afternoon. We should go. Perhaps Askar will be there. In the meantime, we'll check out the address on the notepad."

I looked at the time. "Let's go back to the inn to walk Yukon before we go out again. He's been cooped up for most of the morning."

Chapter 14

We took Yukon for a quick walk, then got back in Shredder's rental and headed north. It was a beautiful sunny day that was supposed to warm up to a downright mild temperature. It would have been fun to spend the entire day at the Santa Festival, but what we were doing was more important.

"Do you think Askar has Rigby stashed somewhere else around here?" I asked as the scenery whizzed by.

"I don't know. The photo of Askar in front of the Santa house is the only lead I have. One of the Santas I spoke to last night said he saw Askar in town that morning, but he wasn't sure where he was staying or if he planned to be around for the entire event. The fact that there was no sign of Rigby in the house seems to indicate that if Askar is still around, he has Rigby stashed somewhere else."

"Are you sure Askar even has him?"

"No. The ransom demand at least made it appear it came from Askar. There's always a possibility he's being set up. The more I think about it, the more I wonder if that isn't actually the case. It doesn't make sense that he'd be hiding out in a town he's known to visit at this time of the year if he was holding someone captive."

"I agree with that."

"If we don't find Rigby at the address I lifted from the notepad, I'm going to call my superiors to discuss the situation in more depth. Things aren't sitting right with me."

When we arrived at the address, we found it belonged to another large house with a barn that must house the horses that were in the pasture just beyond it. The property was impressive, but there was no guard at the gate. Shredder drove past it slowly, then back again. Eventually, he pulled off the road and stopped to consider what to do.

"What do you think?" I asked at last.

"There are cars in the front, so I have to assume there are people on the property. The house looks much like any other; nothing stands out as being a red flag, although there's a large metal building that looks like a warehouse beyond the barn. It could just be storage for hay or farm equipment, but I'd like to check it out to satisfy my curiosity." Shredder looked back at the property. "Maybe you could play damsel in distress again. Knock on the door and tell them your car broke down and that your cell is dead. Ask to use the phone. Meanwhile, I'll head through the woods to the back of the property and take a look inside the building."

"Okay, but no elf costume this time."

"That's fine. I'm going to disable the car in the event that someone decides to check out your story, then head out. Wait five minutes before going up to the house."

I nodded. "Okay. Be careful."

I waited five minutes as instructed, then grabbed my jacket and headed on foot down the road toward the house. I entered the property via the long private drive, knocked on the door, and waited. When no one answered, I knocked again, rang the doorbell, and waited. Still no answer. Despite the cars in the drive, the house seemed to be deserted. Maybe someone was in the barn. I knocked on the door one more time, calling out as I did so. "Hello? Is anyone home? My car's broken down and I need to use a phone."

I waited yet again, but there was no response. I decided to check the barn. I walked across the snow-covered drive and entered the barn through a side door. "Hello," I called out. "Is anyone here?"

Again, there was no answer. I noticed a large door on the side of the barn was open, which would allow the horses in the pasture to come in if they wanted. I supposed they were enjoying the sunshine and unusually warm temperature.

After I left the barn, I headed around the building toward the back, where the building Shredder had said he wanted to check out was located. "Ah ha," I said aloud, and headed that way. I walked around the building until I found an access door, which was unlocked. "Shredder? Are you here?" I called out. The warehouse was huge, reminding me of the metal buildings used at the state fair. A quick glance confirmed that it was mostly empty. There were walls of stacked bales of hay that seemed to be placed strategically around the huge open space, but other than that and a blue and white flag directly in the center, there didn't appear to be anything inside.

I continued inside and was steps away from the blue and white flag when I heard a voice, "Don't move."

I stopped and looked around. "Shredder?"

He appeared from just to my left and slightly behind me. "It seems the building has been mined."

"Mined?"

"I found evidence of land mines surrounding the flag when I first looked in. From the hay bale bunkers and the flag in the middle, I'm assuming this warehouse is used for war games. If that's the case, the land mines are dummies used as part of the simulation. The thing is, I'm not a hundred percent certain my hunch is correct."

"You think I might be standing in the middle of live mines?" I screeched in a high, squeaky voice.

"Probably not, but until I'm a hundred percent sure, I want you to remain absolutely still."

I looked down at my feet and swallowed hard. "I don't see any mines."

"If you look closely, you'll see trip wires and pressure plates that have been camouflaged, but not that well. Just stand still while I figure out what to do."

Okay. Take a deep breath. Don't panic. Panic never helped anyone. "Why didn't you warn me before I got this far?"

"I didn't see you. After I poked my head in here, I headed to the back of the house. By the time I notice you'd come in this direction, you were already through the door. Now stand perfectly still. I'm going to slowly make my way over to you. When I get there, I'll take a closer look. In the meantime, *don't move.*"

I nodded. "I won't move. I promise. But hurry. Wait, don't hurry. Take your time. I'm fine. Really."

Shredder began to move toward me. I focused on my breathing. Slow breath in, slow breath out. Shredder was a pro. He must have done this, or something like it, millions of times. Right? I thought about asking, but I decided I didn't want to know.

I watched as he stepped over trip wires and navigated what looked to be a random path as he made his way toward me. Once he was by my side, he again warned me not to move, and then he slowly bent down. I held my breath while I waited to hear what he had to say next.

"There's a trip wire just in front of you to your left. As long as you don't move your left foot forward, you should be fine with that one. I see a pressure plate behind you to your right. You missed that one narrowly."

"So you're saying as long as I stand here and don't move for the rest of my life, I should be fine."

"Basically." Shredder chuckled.

"Oh my God, did you just *laugh*? I'm probably going to die right here in the middle of this building and you're *laughing*?"

"I'm sorry. And you aren't going to die. As I said, I doubt the mines are real, but just in case they are, I need you to keep doing exactly as I say."

I nodded. "Okay. What do you want me to do?"

"I need you to slide your left foot toward you. Don't lift it off the ground. Just slide it about six inches."

"Okay."

"And Harm, when I say six inches, I mean six inches. No more. Okay?"

I took a deep breath. "I got it. Slide my left foot six inches."

I slowly slid my foot as Shredder had instructed. I'd never been good at spatial equivalencies, so I hoped that wouldn't bite me now. When Shredder told me to stop, I almost jumped, but I didn't.

"Okay," Shredder said. "That was good. Now I want you to take your right foot and lift it off the ground. Lift it straight up. Don't slide it or drag it, just lift it. Once you have it well off the ground, step back at least eighteen inches with that foot only and keep it planted."

"Got it." I took another breath.

"You're doing fine," Shredder said. "Almost there."

I stepped back, then froze. "Okay, now what?"

"Transfer your weight to your right leg so you can lift your left foot off the ground. What I want you to do is to bring your left foot next to your right foot without dragging it along the ground."

I had to smile at that. It was a nervous smile, but a smile nonetheless. "It just occurred to me that all those hours I spent playing Twister with Chloe as a kid was training for this moment."

"I guess it was." Shredder smiled back at me.

By the time my feet were side by side on the ground, I was certain I was going to throw up.

"One more step," Shredder said. "Take your right foot and step directly to your right. Move your foot about a foot. Once your right foot is planted, move your left foot next to it. Don't move forward or backward at all. This is a parallel step. Got it?"

"I got it."

I did as Shredder said. Once I was in the clear, Shredder pulled me into his arms for the longest and tightest hug I'd ever experienced.

"I did it," I said when Shredder finally pulled back. "We did it."

Shredder hugged me again.

"Now what?" I asked.

Shredder went outside and came back with a large rock. He tossed it onto one of the pressure plates. There was a loud bang and a puff of dust, but nothing even close to a deadly explosion. "It looks like the mines are dummies, as I suspected."

It was then that I noticed a very large man walking toward us with a very large rifle in his hands. "It looks like we're busted," I said under my breath.

"The two of you know this is private property?" the man asked.

I had no idea how to respond, so I looked at Shredder.

"I'm sorry," Shredder said. "My name is Chris Stone and this is my wife, Claudia. We were on our way to Tinseltown for the festival when our car broke down. We hoped to use your phone to call for a tow, but when we knocked on the door to the house, no one answered."

"We saw the cars, so we figured someone might be around, so we checked out the barn," I added.

"Which is when I noticed the metal building," Shredder continued. "I'm afraid my curiosity got the better of me and I went over to check it out. I'll pay for any damage."

The man narrowed his gaze and paused, as if trying to decide what to make of us. "I guess there was no harm done. I thought I heard the doorbell, but I was in the basement and not expecting anyone, so I didn't bother to answer. If you still need to use the phone, follow me back to the house."

"We'd appreciate that very much," Shredder said.

I fell into step next to him and walked to the house next to the man, who was still clutching his rifle.

"What's up with that building anyway?" I asked. "Not that it's any of my business, but I'm curious."

"War games."

I lifted a brow. "War games?"

"I'm part of a group that participates in role-playing games. We divide up and use paint guns instead of real ones and pretend to have battles. During the summer months, the games begin outdoors with two teams each intent on getting in to the warehouse and capturing the flag. The mines, which provide a loud bang but are basically harmless, are part of the experience. The whole thing might sound silly to you, but it's actually a very demanding simulation that challenges a man both intellectually and physically."

"It doesn't sound silly at all," I said, then glanced at Shredder. "At least not any sillier than dressing up as Santa and his elf, which is what we were on our way to do."

The man chuckled and showed Shredder to the phone. He made his call and then we thanked the man and went back to the car.

"Do you buy all that?" I asked after Shredder called the tow company back to cancel the pickup. I'd asked Shredder why he hadn't just faked the call to a tow company, and he'd said it was best to stay true to our story in case the man checked his phone records.

"It may seem odd, but war games are fairly popular. He has an elaborate setup, but if you have the time, money, and interest, why not go all-in and build an elaborate field of battle?"

"I wonder why this address was on the notepad in the house where you think Askar might be staying."

"Maybe he or whoever owns the house is into role-playing," Shredder answered.

"Maybe. Of course, if Rigby really isn't in the house, we're back to square one."

"I wish we could have gotten a look inside," Shredder said. "It didn't seem like the sort of place one would keep a prisoner, but the man admitted to hearing you ring the doorbell and ignoring it, and he admitted to being in the basement. I wonder what he was doing down there."

"Do you think that's where he has Rigby?" I asked.

"I don't know, but I'd like to figure out a way to find out."

We headed directly to the inn when we got back to town. We needed to be at the parade in less than an hour, but I thought both of us needed to regroup.

"I sort of feel like we've been led on a wild-goose chase," I said after I kicked off my boots and curled up in front of the fire.

"I agree. It's as if this entire trip has been nothing but a huge diversion."

"Diversion from what?" I wondered.

Shredder creased his forehead. "I'm not sure. I feel like a dog chasing his tail, and I don't like it in the least."

"Do you think the photo of Askar was faked?"

"No. He's been seen in town. I think he is or at least was here, and it's possible someone snapped his picture. I'm beginning to wonder if the ransom demand was faked, however."

"Why would anyone fake a ransom demand?"

"I don't know, but the more I think about it, the more I realize something isn't lining up."

"Okay," I said after stifling a yawn. "What isn't working for you?"

Shredder began pacing around the room. From the pinched expression on his face, I could see he was deep in thought. Then he said, "If Askar kidnapped Rigby and was holding him for ransom, why would he be hanging out in Tinseltown, where he's known to visit at this time of the year every year? If he really had a prisoner, it makes more sense that he'd hold him in a location where no one would think to look."

"Agreed."

"And why would Askar be interested in the Turkish prisoners anyway? Yes, he was born in Turkey, but he didn't spend that much time there, and as far as I know, while he's known for handling criminal tasks for other people, he doesn't seem to have any real political ties. He accepts jobs based on money alone."

"About that: If he's a known criminal, why isn't he in prison?"

"He's too good to leave evidence behind. His reputation is well known, but no one has been able to prove he's done anything it's rumored he's responsible for. Because he works internationally and moves around a lot, it's been hard for anyone to nail him down."

"He comes here every year, so he can't be impossible to nail down," I said.

"Good point. I guess if anyone ever does come up with proof Askar actually did any of the things he's supposed to have done, we'll know where to find him. At least in December. At this point, however, I'm just not buying the fact that he has Rigby. If I had to guess, I'd say the actual kidnapper is using Askar to create a diversion. I'm going to call in to my team. I think we may need to widen our assumptions to include a scenario where someone other than Askar might have kidnapped Rigby. I'm not sure the two Turkish prisoners are even the real objective."

"What now?" I asked Shredder after he hung up.

"I've been given until the end of the day tomorrow to try to confirm or deny Rigby's detainment by Askar. Whether I find proof one way or the other, I'm to head out on another assignment by Friday."

"The folks you work for aren't real big on time off for the holiday."

Shredder chuckled. "Not at all. It's fine, though. I like to stay busy."

"So do you have a plan to find Askar?"

Shredder nodded. "I do. From what I found in the house where we suspect Askar is staying, it appears he plans to attend the parade. We should as well."

"If we find him, then what? Do you think he'll talk to us?"

Shredder shrugged. "He might. If he doesn't have Rigby, he probably won't want the hassle of having everyone thinking he does. In that case, I'd think he'd be motivated to get things cleared up. If he does have Rigby, he'll probably want to know what's going on with his ransom demand."

Chapter 15

We decided to take Yukon to the parade with us. I wanted to take him for a good long walk anyway, and I knew he'd enjoy the hustle and bustle of all the people crowded along the sidewalks framing the narrow street. Denali would have hated the crowds, but Yukon was definitely a people person. Shredder and I walked up and down the sidewalks for a good twenty minutes before we spotted Askar. He was dressed in a Santa suit and standing next to a sleigh on runners that looked as if it was going to be pulled by two caribou. He was chatting with a woman dressed as an elf. It would seem he was about to play the part of Santa Claus himself, riding through town in the sleigh at the end of the parade. Somehow, a man who'd be interested in doing such a thing didn't meld in my mind with someone who was known as an international criminal and killer.

"What now?" I asked when Shredder pointed him out to me.

"Wait here with Yukon. I'll be back in a few minutes."

I wanted to argue but didn't. Shredder was the spy; I was just the sidekick. Askar might be more apt to talk with Shredder if I wasn't around. I watched as Shredder approached him and said something, which was followed by Askar chuckling quite loudly. That got Yukon's attention, and he began to growl.

"It's okay," I said to him, ruffling him behind the ears.

I continued to watch the exchange, focusing in to see if I could pick up any images, but nothing came to me. After they'd been talking for maybe fifteen minutes, Shredder returned to my side. There was a confused expression on his face.

"What did he say?"

"He said he was in Tinseltown to attend the event and wasn't holding Rigby."

"So is that it? Did he say anything else?"

Shredder frowned and looked me in the eye. "He suggested Rigby might not have been abducted."

"What do you mean? Your team received the video. Right?"

Shredder nodded. "When Askar first suggested the entire kidnapping scheme was a ruse, I thought he was just trying to provide a distraction, but the more I think about it, the more I think he might very well be right."

I pulled Yukon closer to my side as a group of teenage boys ran past us. "You might need to walk me through this."

"Askar suggested that Rigby might be the one who set up the kidnapping story as a decoy."

"But why?"

"When Rigby was sent to the inn to meet Reggie in the place of Deidrick Eckhart, he was given a lot of money, all in cash."

"Why not do a bank transfer?"

"Remember, the point of the exchange was to launder cash by investing it in legitimate business ventures. In this case, the money would most likely have been used to fund the projects under development by Drake Weston's company. Up to this point, I've suspected that Rigby was made by Gershwin, but what if he wasn't? What if Rigby killed Reggie and faked his own kidnapping to make off with the money? Everyone has been looking for Askar, but no one has been looking for the money."

"If Rigby stole the money, why did he want everyone to think he'd been kidnapped by Askar? Why did he make the ransom demand?"

"As you so eloquently suggested, he was stalling. Maybe he needed time to get himself and all that cash out of the country. I need to make another call." Shredder grabbed my hand and pulled Yukon and me onto a much quieter side street. From the first few words out of his mouth, I realized he'd called his superiors to run this crazy new theory past them. Shredder went over the series of events regarding Rigby's kidnapping in great detail while I listened in. On Monday late afternoon, they'd received a video recorded by Rigby. In it, he said he'd been detained by Askar, who was demanding the release of two Turkish prisoners in exchange for his life. There was no one else in the video, nor was Rigby physically bound, although he was sporting a fairly significant black eye. The video had been routed through a series of international servers, so there was no way to verify from where it originated. Could Rigby have recorded the video himself? Shredder's superiors seemed to believe he could have.

The only other communications supposedly received from Askar had been in the form of emails, sent to the same email address from which the video had originated. Because the source of the email was unknown, Shredder's superiors again admitted it was possible they might not have been negotiating with Askar. The part that really didn't make sense was Rigby naming Askar in the first place. It seemed that by doing so, if he had indeed been behind the whole thing himself, he was taking a risk that Askar would be found and his story would be refuted. Normally, Askar was as slippery as an eel and almost impossible to pin down, so perhaps Rigby hadn't known he was in Alaska. Or perhaps he had known, and Askar was in on Rigby's plot.

When Shredder mentioned the money, the people he worked for, or with were suddenly very interested in what had become of it.

"What did they say?" I asked after Shredder hung up.

"From what I presented, the people I work for agreed Askar most likely isn't involved in Rigby's disappearance. They're giving real consideration to the possibility that Rigby may have faked his own kidnapping. They have eyes and ears on airports, seaports, and borders. They'll find him. Eventually."

"So where does that leave us?" I asked.

"I take you back to Rescue and head out for my next assignment."

Well, how frustrating was that! To be assigned to a mission and then relieved of it before it came to its conclusion seemed downright unbearable to me.

"Are we leaving today?" I was torn as to whether leaving now was the smartest thing to do.

"We can go in the morning if you'd prefer. I don't have to report for my next assignment until Friday. Or I can take you home right now. It's up to you."

I looked out toward the lights that had seemed so festive less than an hour before. Somehow, when I looked at them now, I found them depressing. "Let's head back. You can stay in my guest room tonight. I'm sure Denali would love to spend some time with you. We can pick him up from Jake's on the way home."

I called Serena to let her know my training had gotten over early and I'd be home that evening. She was welcome to leave whenever she wanted. I assured her I'd take care of the animal-related evening chores; she didn't need to worry about a thing. It would be good to be home in my own cabin with the animals, but I couldn't help but feel a little sad and a lot frustrated.

I hadn't brought a lot with me, so it didn't take me long to pack. Less than thirty minutes after making the decision to leave, Shredder and I were on the road.

"If Rigby did take off with the money, where do you think he'd go? It would be hard to board a commercial flight with that much cash, so he'd need to either charter a private jet or maybe drive. But if he chose to drive, there's the border crossing to deal with. Seems risky." I paused as I pondered the question. "How did Reggie do it? If he took possession of the dirty money, how did he plan to get it back to Seattle?"

"He hired a private jet when he traveled for business. I suppose it makes sense that Rigby would have hired one as well."

"I wonder if we can figure out who he hired. If he wanted a quick getaway, it seems like he would have hired someone local."

"There are a lot of private air charters in Alaska. You could ask your friend Dani to ask around. She probably knows all the local players."

I took out my phone. "That's a good idea. I'll call her right now."

Dani agreed to make some calls and would let me know what she'd found out by the end of the night. She'd never actually met or even seen Rigby, so I provided a description in the event someone had been hired by a single male passenger in the past two days. I knew Dani must be curious about what was going on, but to her credit, she didn't pry. At least she didn't pry over the phone. The next time I saw her in person might be another story.

"Do you really think Rigby killed Reggie?" I asked after I hung up the phone.

"If he's done what we now suspect, then yes. He would need to get Reggie out of the way."

"Do you think he killed Piney Portman too?" I added.

Shredder adjusted his hands on the steering wheel. "I don't think so. From what you folks dug up, I think Reggie killed Piney."

"Yeah," I agreed. "It does seem so," I sat in silence for several minutes. "If we find out Rigby's innocent, and he really was abducted, who do you think might have taken him?"

Shredder drummed his fingers on the steering wheel. "The demand for the release of the Turkish prisoners doesn't seem to fit anyone's agenda. Not even Askar's. Which is partially why I believe Askar isn't behind whatever's going on."

"Have you known Rigby long?"

Shredder shook his head. "Long enough to be surprised that he'd do what it appears he may have done. On the other hand…"

"On the other hand?" I asked.

"Looking back, it does seem Rigby spent a lot of time complaining about what he considered to be a crappy salary given the danger we put ourselves in on a daily basis."

I turned so I could see the silhouette of Shredder's face. "Do you agree? Is what you're paid insufficient given the nature of the job?"

"Perhaps. What we do is dangerous and difficult. I'm not sure it would be possible to place a dollar amount on the worth of the missions we undertake. And even if it was possible to monetize the risk, and it was determined we were underpaid, it wouldn't matter to me and most of the men and women I work with. We do it for the glory."

"What glory?" I laughed. "No one even knows what you do."

Shredder smiled. "True. But if not for the glory, for the sense of satisfaction it provides. It's hard to describe how it feels to be assigned to go out to save the world and then do it."

I raised a brow. "Save the world?"

Shredder turned to glance at me. "At times."

Saying you saved the world was somewhat grandiose, but in Shredder's case, I actually believed him.

The conversation dropped off and we rode in silence. It was nice to have a minute to gather my thoughts. Was it really less than a week until Christmas? I still had quite a lot to do. It was a good thing I was coming home early. I wanted to get a tree, now that I had lights and decorations, and I still needed to buy a few gifts. Houston and Harley had agreed to come to the Christmas Eve dinner at Jake's, so I wanted to be sure to have small gifts for them. I was sad Shredder couldn't stay for that, but I understood why he couldn't. I was so focused on my plans for the next few days, I didn't notice the beep that let me know I had a text.

"Your phone is beeping," Shredder said.

I picked it up and looked at it. "Dani found the pilot Rigby hired. According to Dani, a pilot she knows, Darian Green, flew Rigby to Los Angeles."

"Damn," Shredder said. "A part of me was really hoping we were wrong and he was innocent. Oh well; at least I know where to pick up his trail."

Chapter 16

Thursday, December 20

Once he had verification of where Rigby was last seen, Shredder was off in the wind. He took me home, gave me a long hug goodbye, then drove away into the night. I knew he was the sort to come and go almost without notice, but I was going to miss him. Of course, as depressed as I was about his quick disappearance from our lives, Denali was even more bummed. I had no idea how he could know he was gone for good, but somehow he seemed to know. I decided we could both use some fun, so I called Houston to ask if he was up for the tree-cutting expedition we'd talked about. He was having a slow day and agreed to meet me at my cabin. I told him to bring Kojak because I planned to bring my entire canine crew.

"And Shredder works for some secret black ops division of the military or the government or something, but you aren't exactly sure which?" Houston asked after I took Jake's advice and filled him in on at least part of what I knew.

"Correct. He has connections everywhere and knows a lot of people. I think he must be pretty high up on the hierarchy, although I'm not sure which hierarchy we're talking about. What I do know is that he's a great guy with a good heart who Denali adores, so he must be pure of heart. I don't know him well at all, except that on two occasions he's popped into my life for a few days, taken me on an adventure, and left."

Houston picked up a stick and tossed it for the dogs. "He sounds like an interesting guy. I hope he comes back so I can meet him."

"Yeah," I said, feeling that tug of sadness. "Me too. He's doing what he wants to do, but I feel bad for him. He doesn't seem to live anywhere or have anyone in his life. At least not anyone who isn't a colleague. It seems lonely."

"It does, but for some men the mission is the most important thing. They're willing to give up quite a lot to do the job they believe they were called to do."

I reached down and stroked Honey's head. "Yeah, I get that. I do wish that after all we tried to do to put all the pieces together, we had more closure. I assume Shredder will eventually track down Rigby, but it would have been a lot more satisfying to be in on the capture. And then there are the unanswered questions about Reggie and Piney's murders, and whether they're connected to Rigby. Shredder thinks Reggie killed Piney, but without proof…"

"Actually, we do have proof," Houston said. "While you and Shredder were off looking for Rigby,

I continued to do my job. I had the jacket Reggie was wearing on the day of the ski trip tested, and the guys at the lab were able to identify a stain found on the front as being blood. Piney's blood. Combined with everything else we know, I think we can say Reggie killed Piney. I'm still trying to work out who killed Reggie, but from everything you just told me, this Rigby sounds like a good suspect."

"I thought so as well until Dani informed me that Darian picked Rigby up at the airport at one o'clock on Monday. It was more like two thirty when Reggie died."

Houston groaned. "Damn. I thought we had that one wrapped up."

"Afraid not," I said. I stopped walking and looked around. "I was thinking after we tromped all the way out here, we should get two trees. One for my place and one for yours."

Houston raised a brow. "Mine? Is this outing really an attempt to sneak some Christmas cheer into my life?"

I shrugged. "Maybe. Is it working?"

Houston laughed. "Yes, I guess it is. A small tree might be nice. I guess I should do something to celebrate the holiday because I don't plan to travel home."

"If you aren't going home, you should come to Neverland for Christmas Eve. Jake closes at noon and Sarge cooks a big dinner for the entire search-and-rescue team. Dogs are welcome, as are guests of the team. Harley is coming, and so is Chloe, and I'm pretty sure Wyatt is bringing the girl he's been dating, who I'm very excited to meet. So how about it? Are you in?"

Houston hesitated.

"It beats a TV dinner. And Kojak will have fun with the other dogs. If you don't want to do it for yourself, do it for him."

"Okay," Houston said. "That sounds nice. Should I bring anything?"

"Just your stretchy pants. You'll be glad you have them when you see all the food Sarge's making."

Houston stopped walking in front of a small but perfectly shaped tree. "How about this one?"

"I think that one is lovely." I stood back as Houston chopped it down. "One down and one to go." I glanced into the distance. "I seem to remember there being a grove of pretty little trees just over that hill."

Houston laid the tree he'd just cut on the sled we'd brought. "Lead the way. If we're lucky, we'll be home before the sun starts to set." Houston picked up the rope and began pulling the sled. "I don't see how I'll ever get used to these short days."

"I'm not sure you do. I've lived here my whole life and at times, I think I'll go crazy during the shortest days of the year."

Houston, the dogs, and I trudged over the little hill. The trees I'd been heading for were right where I remembered, but I noticed something else as well. Sleigh tracks. "You know, the one clue we really haven't resolved regarding Reggie's murder are the tracks we found near the body. Shredder and I followed them to a house a couple of miles from the murder site, but no one was home, and then we got the lead that took us to Tinseltown and never followed up on it."

"I talked to the man who lives in the house at the end of the trail, Gavin White. He was out for a ride on the day before the murder, which would explain the tracks, but he swore he had nothing to do with Reggie's death."

My eyes grew big. "The tracks couldn't have been from the day before. I specifically remember it snowed Monday morning: heavy snow and large flakes. If he was in the area the day before, the tracks would have been covered or at least mostly covered by the time we found them on Monday afternoon."

Houston took out his ax and went to work on the tree I pointed out before he answered. "Now that you mention the snow, I remember it too. It sounds like another chat with the guy is in order. Let's take these trees and the dogs back to your place and go over to have a conversation with him. I didn't get the vibe that he was lying when I spoke to him, but I didn't remember that it snowed, and I definitely don't have your skill as a lie detector. If he killed Reggie, we can wrap this whole thing up."

******

After Houston and I left the trees and dogs at my cabin, we went by road to the house Shredder and I had found after following the sled tracks. There was a truck in the drive, so I assumed he was home. My heart quickened just a bit as Houston unsnapped his holster and checked the status of his gun.

"What's the plan?" I asked.

"I'd like to take a look around, but I don't have a warrant or a reason to get one, so I can't force it. I'll just go to the door and have a conversation with him, see how it goes." Houston looked at me. "Maybe you should wait here until I can get a feel for how he'll react to further interrogation."

I was about to argue but I realized I could take a look in the barn while Houston interviewed him. "Okay," I said. "Give me a holler if you need me."

Houston got out and walked to the front door. I slipped out of his SUV and crouched down low. I watched as he went up to the door and knocked. The porch light went on. I stayed where I was until the door opened to reveal a tall, broad-shouldered man. After a few seconds, he opened the door and Houston went inside. As soon as the door closed, I ran across the clearing to the barn. I wasn't sure exactly what I was looking for, but I hoped something would stand out. I only needed one thing that definitively tied him to Reggie; that should be enough for Houston to get the warrant he needed. Or at least I imagined it would. I didn't know much about police work.

The corral behind the barn contained four caribou. They appeared to be healthy, well-cared-for animals. I went to the back of the barn, where I found a tarp thrown over two things. Both were sleighs. I didn't suppose there was any crime in owning two sleighs, but I didn't remember either sleigh or any of the reindeer being here when Shredder and I looked around. I supposed the owner of the house could have been out with one of the teams because he hadn't been around either, but I wondered who'd been out in the second sleigh.

I hoped to have more time to look around, but I heard Houston come out of the house only minutes after he'd entered. He paused on the porch to talk to the homeowner, so I hurried back to the SUV. When he joined me, I said what was foremost in my mind. "There are two sleighs in the barn and four caribou in the pen. Both the tracks we found when we were looking for Nick and the ones we found near Reggie's body consisted of a single set of sleigh tracks and prints from two caribou. When Shredder and I were here, the place was empty. Neither sleigh and none of the reindeer were on the property. Assuming the man you just spoke to was out with one team, who was with the other?"

Houston frowned. "Two sleighs. Are you sure?"

"I just saw them with my own eyes."

"I thought you were going to wait in the vehicle."

"I lied. Look, I know I didn't do as you asked, but this might be important. Did you ask him about Nick Clauston?"

"I did, and he said he found him wandering around on Saturday morning. At first, Nick didn't remember who he was, so White decided to bring him home to try to jog his memory. Once Nick remembered who he was, White gave him a ride back to the inn."

"Did you ask him why he didn't call you?"

Houston nodded. "He said initially, he thought Nick might have been on drugs. He didn't want to get him in trouble; he just wanted to sober him up. Once he realized he had some sort of mental problem, he felt bad for him. When Nick finally remembered he'd been staying at the inn, White thought he'd just drop him off and let him go in on his own. He said Nick was upset, afraid his daughter would be angry for causing him trouble. He knew some family members didn't deal well with that sort of disease and he wanted to leave the man with some dignity, rather than taking him inside like a disobedient child. He wasn't anticipating he'd take a seat in the swing, but in the end, it all worked out."

I took a moment to look at the house. "That shows compassion and sensitivity. Even Nick made it sound as if the man who brought him home was very nice to him. Killing Reggie, however, is not so nice." I looked toward the barn. "Two sleighs, two men. One nice and one not so nice."

Houston put his hand on the door handle. "I'll go find out who the second sleigh belongs to."

I waited impatiently for Houston to return. I wasn't good at waiting, and it seemed I'd been doing a lot of it lately. I watched as Houston stood on the porch and chatted with the man. They went inside again. After a few more minutes, Houston stepped back out onto the porch and shook the man's hand, then headed back to the SUV.

"Well?" I asked.

"White said the second sleigh and the two additional caribou belong to a buddy of his named Joey, who lives north of here. The roof on Joey's barn caved in, so he's allowing him to use his barn until it's fixed. I asked him if the second sleigh had been taken out on Monday. A friend of Joey's was by to borrow it. White wasn't home at the time and didn't even know the friend had borrowed the team until this morning. I asked him if he knew the friend's name. He didn't, so he called Joey while I waited. The man who borrowed the team is named Nicolas."

"Nicolas Askar?" I asked.

Chapter 17

Monday, December 24

After a very long week, I awoke on Christmas Eve morning to a fresh coat of snow and a cabin full of animals, which made me happy. I pulled the covers up to my chin as I contemplated dragging myself out of bed. I knew the animals needed to be tended to, but a few more minutes wouldn't hurt. The past few days had been hectic and somewhat trying, and I felt as if I deserved to sleep in just a bit on this very special morning.

I rolled over on my side to check on the dogs who slept on the floor next to me, only to find the room totally devoid of dogs. I frowned. How had they gotten out of the bedroom? And then I smelled the coffee. Jake? We were getting together later and I thought he would have spent the morning with Jordan, but I couldn't think of anyone else who would simply walk into my cabin and make coffee. Unless...

I slipped my legs over the side of the bed and slid out. I pulled on my robe and slippers and headed out to the living area, to find Shredder sitting on my sofa, sipping coffee with a pile of dogs on either side of him.

"What are you doing here?"

"Merry Christmas to you as well."

I let out a half laugh. "Merry Christmas, Shredder. And while I'm very happy to see you, I need to know why I'm seeing you. Do you have another mission in Alaska?"

Shredder reached out and scrubbed his hand through Denali's thick mane. "Not a mission. More like a day off on the way to a new mission."

I walked into the kitchen and poured my own cup of coffee. "A new mission? Did you wrap up the old one?"

Shredder nodded. "Sort of. I managed to catch up with Rigby, who is in a heap of trouble. He is in custody and will most likely be there for a very long time. I had a chance to speak to him as I escorted him to detention, and he admitted he hired Askar to kill Reggie after Reggie figured out he wasn't really Eckhart."

"And Askar?"

"In the wind. Not surprising, given that we gave him a huge head start."

I sat down on the sofa. "I can't believe we had him and we let him go."

"Don't feel bad. The man is crafty. He gave us Rigby, which sent us off after him and gave Askar a chance to disappear. The fact that he's crafty is one of the reasons he's never been brought to justice. I should have known he was behind Reggie's death when I found out about the accuracy used to slit his throat. Askar is known as an efficient and merciful killer."

I thought of the sensation I'd shared with Reggie of his last moment. The pain in his throat and his struggle to breathe. I supposed there were worse ways to die, but I don't think I'd label the man's death as merciful.

"Are you here all day?" I asked, smiling at the look of delight on Denali's face.

"I should head out this evening. I don't want to interrupt any plans you might have."

"I don't have plans. At least not until I have to leave for dinner at the bar. You can come along if you want."

Shredder looked like he might actually be considering it, then he shook his head. "I should probably head out before dinner. But I'd love to go for a walk with you and the kids. If you were planning on taking a walk, that is."

I glanced around the room filled with my furry family. "I take a walk every morning whether I'm in the mood or not. Just let me get dressed."

******

"I can't believe how much progress you've made with this little guy in just a little over a week," I said to Harley later that evening, after he showed up at Neverland with Brando. "He really seems to listen to you."

"It took a day or two, but we managed to come to an understanding. He agreed not to chew on everything in sight and I agreed to let him sleep in the bed with me."

"Sounds like an agreement that benefits you both. How's he doing with the bathroom training?"

"He hasn't had any accidents. I think the guy who dropped him off must have kept him locked up in the house without regular trips outdoors. I haven't had a single issue in that area." Harley looked at me with a smile on his face. "I know I said I wasn't interested in adopting him, but if you and I can work out a few details, I might consider it."

"That would be great. Whatever you need."

"I'd like to have you continue to work with both of us on the training, and I'll need somewhere to leave him when I can't take him with me when I leave town. I don't plan to do as many movies or to travel as much, but there will be times when I'll be on the set for weeks at a time, and having a dog to see to then isn't always doable."

I wrapped my arms around Harley's neck and gave him a hug. "I totally agree to both conditions. Congratulations, Harley. You're going to be an amazing dad."

Harley grinned. "You know, part of me has always wanted to be a dad." He looked down at the puppy, who obviously adored him. "I'm going to take him out before dinner."

When Harley left, I looked around the room. I felt a warmth in my heart as I took in the perfection of Jake's decorations, the friends who I considered family, and the dogs who meant so very, very much to me. Life was good. At times, life was hard, but in the end, I decided, it was also perfect.

I was debating the idea of refilling my wineglass when I noticed Houston wandering across the room with a wrapped package in his hand.

"For me?" I asked when he thrust it toward me.

"It's just a small token. I wanted to thank you for helping me through Christmas. As I've indicated, it isn't my favorite holiday."

"Bad breakup?" I asked.

He hesitated. He glanced around the room and then back at me. "I don't like to talk about it, but my mother was murdered on Christmas when I was eight."

I gasped. "Murdered? What happened?"

"It was Christmas Eve. I'd been put to bed, but I was so excited for Santa to arrive that I snuck downstairs. My dad was a cop and he was working that evening, although Mom had assured me that he'd be home for Christmas morning. Mom was in the kitchen baking pies, so I snuck over to the tree to look at all the brightly wrapped packages. At some point, I heard her come into the room, so I slipped under the tree. I arranged the packages just so. I was pretty sure Mom couldn't see me. I remember looking up through the branches at the colorful lights. I remember being so happy and so excited."

So far, Houston's memory was a lot like mine had been, but I was soon to learn that his deviated at that point.

"There was a sound on the porch," Houston continued. "At first I thought it might be my dad, but then I realized he always parked around the back and came in through the kitchen. From my hiding place beneath the tree, I watched as my mother went to the door. She opened it and gasped. For a minute, I thought maybe Santa had come early. She seemed so surprised. But then I heard a tiny gasp, which was followed by a tiny little cry as her breath escaped her lips for the very last time."

I gasped. "Someone killed her right there on the porch?"

Houston nodded. "Someone strangled her. I saw her fall to the ground and I froze. By the time I finally had the presence of mind to climb out from under the tree, she was dead and the person who'd killed her was gone."

"What did you do?"

"I called my dad. The rest is a blur. My grandmother came and picked me and my sister up. My dad said it would just be for a few days, but we both stayed with her until we went to college."

"Your dad didn't want you to come home?"

"He didn't deal well with what happened. At first, he was driven to find the person who killed my mom and worked around the clock for several years. But when he couldn't find the person who killed the love of his life, he sort of lost it. He started drinking and eventually lost his job. He died in a car accident when I was sixteen."

I took Houston's hand in mine. "I'm so very sorry. Here I've been, trying to thrust Christmas on you, when the reason you aren't a fan of the holiday is so horrific, I don't even know what to say. I feel awful."

"Don't." Houston squeezed my hand. "What happened was awful, but it was a long time ago. I've realized during the past week that it's time to move on. I can't change what happened, but I can use my mom's death to help me to be a better man. I became a cop because of her murder, and as a cop, I've done a lot of good. I realized when you brought me that little tree for my office that my mom loved Christmas. It would make her incredibly sad that I stopped celebrating. I guess that little tree gave me the push I needed to deal with my memories and move on. It's what my mom would want for me."

I put my arms around Houston's neck and gave him a hard, long hug. "I'm glad the little tree helped. If there's ever anything I can do for you, if there's some way I can help, please just let me know."

"I will," Houston said. "I still haven't tracked down my mom's killer. I've had a few false leads over the years that never panned out. I haven't given up, though, and am still working on it. I have some feelers out, and I feel like I'm getting close. How close, I'm not certain. The leads I'm working on may not go anywhere, but there may come a time I'll call on you and your superpower to help find the person I've spent my entire adult life looking for."

"If that time comes, I'll do what I can."

I looked at the room filled with all the people I loved. These people had helped me heal after my parents' death and even more so after Val's. They'd helped me to get my answers and find closure. And damn if I wasn't going to find a way to do the same for Houston. Maybe not today, maybe not even this year. But someday.

USA Today best-selling author Kathi Daley lives in beautiful Lake Tahoe with her husband Ken. When she isn't writing, she likes spending time hiking the miles of desolate trails surrounding her home. She has authored more than a hundred and fifty books in thirteen series. Find out more about her books at www.kathidaley.com

Printed in Great Britain
by Amazon